Sophie Washington
Mismatch

by

Tonya Duncan Ellis

Other Books by
Tonya Duncan Ellis

Sophie Washington: Queen of the Bee

Sophie Washington: The Snitch

Sophie Washington:
Things You Didn't Know About Sophie

Sophie Washington: The Gamer

Sophie Washington: Hurricane

Sophie Washington: Mission: Costa Rica

Sophie Washington: Secret Santa

Sophie Washington: Code One

Table of Contents

Chapter 1

Tryouts

I'm trying out for the tennis team with my friends, and I feel like I'm on my way to get a flu shot. This is my first time playing on an actual sports team, and I'm as jittery as a bucking bronco before the rodeo.

"You need to move faster, Sophie," says my best friend Chloe, "or we'll be late."

"Yeah, come on," says my other bestie, Mariama. "You're moving like your feet are glued to the ground."

The three of us walk to Xavier's athletic complex and turn left by the baseball fields. Our private school built the sports center that includes a track, tennis courts, and baseball and soccer fields two years ago, and everything in it is state-of-the-art.

As we push through the metal gate onto the tennis courts, I see the other girls who are trying out. My stomach feels tight, and my hands are so sweaty I almost drop my tennis racket.

Lindsey, Jacqueline and Kennedy, all eighth graders, talk like they've known each other since their Dora the Explorer days.

"This YouTube video is hilarious!" Kennedy says with a giggle as she shows the two other girls her cell phone.

"Let me see." Lindsey pushes her long blonde bangs out of her eyes to get a better view.

"Hi, guys!" says Chloe as we walk up.

The three older girls don't say anything, and Kennedy looks us up and down.

Chloe already appears like a tennis pro in her matching pleated, red, and white tennis skirt and top. Her shiny black curls are held back with a cute bow, and she carries a fancy new tennis racket. I'm guessing Mariama's mom, a sewing expert, made the pretty pink shorts outfit she's wearing that has interesting zebra print cutouts sewn in. Mariama's family moved to Houston from Nigeria, Africa, last year, and she loves to wear clothes that show off her culture. I'm sporting our school's P.E. shorts and tee shirt, and a baseball cap covers my two thick braids.

"Hey! That video must be interesting," Chloe continues, not noticing the other girls' cold stares. "Watcha looking at?"

"Something too grown up for a little sixth grader like you," Kennedy says, breaking the silence. "It's PG-13."

"That's a good one, Ken," says Jacqueline with a laugh.

If some eighth graders said something like that to me, I'd want to curl into a ball and disappear, but Chloe doesn't back down a bit.

"Sorry, nobody told us it was National Mean Girl Day," she says. "Come on, Sophie and Mariama. Let's wait over there."

"See ya, wouldn't want to be ya," says Kennedy as we head over to the chain link fence that surrounds the tennis courts. The older girls turn back to scrolling through their phones.

"Wonder what her deal is?" I say to my friends.

"She thinks she's 'Miss It' because she's played tennis since third grade and is really good," says Mariama. "She was team captain last year."

"Well, with girls like that on the tennis team, no wonder not many are here for tryouts," says Chloe.

"Yeah, they sure know how to make you feel unwelcome," I say.

Most of the other middle school girls run track or play softball, so I heard that Coach Quackenbush lets practically everyone who tries out be on the tennis team. That's good news for me because I can hit the ball back when it comes directly to my racket, but I'm not going to be bringing home a first-place trophy anytime soon. So far, there's only us and the eighth graders here, so my chances of actually making the team seem high.

When Chloe suggested we try out, I was excited about playing on my first real sports team with my friends. New players are usually partnered up to play doubles at our school, and I figured I would be matched with either Chloe, Mariama, or our other good friend, Valentina. I even made up a cool, secret handshake that my partner and I can do when we make points.

"Too bad Valentina can't tryout," says Mariama. "She'd have told that mean Kennedy a thing or two."

Someone spilled popcorn on the gym floor during our last home basketball game of the season a couple of weeks ago, just as Valentina, our cheer captain, was doing a front walkover. She slipped and crashed on the floor, spraining her ankle, and she has to wear a medical boot for the next six weeks. Now she can't try out with us, and our friend group is uneven. If the coach doesn't pair me with Chloe or Mariama, I'm not sure who I'll be playing with.

While we wait for Coach Quackenbush to arrive, I notice Mackenzie Clark, another sixth grader, swatting a ball on the ground with her racket on the other end of the tennis courts. She's wearing ear buds and has her back to us, so she probably didn't hear what just happened with the eighth graders.

I've never spoken to Mackenzie, because she's not too friendly. Her skin is a ghostly white, her hair is styled in a short, spiky cut, and dyed a blackish blue color, and she sometimes wears black nail polish. Mackenzie keeps to herself, and she's always in detention for being late to school or missing class. Her father owns a popular, fast food restaurant that makes really good hamburgers. Since she used to be chubby in elementary school, some of the meaner kids in our class started calling Mackenzie "Big Mac." Unfortunately for her, the name has stuck even though she's slimmed down as she's gotten taller.

"Here comes Coach Quackenbush!" Chloe points out the short, bald man with turned out feet and a beige polo shirt. "Tryouts are just one day. I wonder if we'll find out who are partners are at the end?"

Holding a clipboard in his hand, the coach waddles over to us with his lips puckered out.

"Welcome to the tennis team, ladies. All right, let's get started."

Chapter 2

Mismatch

Findley Peterson, a seventh grader, who was on the tennis team last year, warned us about "The Quacker."

"Don't be late to practice or he'll have the entire team run laps," she said. "And never let him catch you talking when he's explaining something. He'll ask you questions about it in front of *everybody*."

I learn the second warning the hard way when I whisper to Chloe while the Coach is teaching us about hitting volley shots. "Where'd you buy your tennis outfit?"

"All right, Miss Washington, can you tell the team what a volley is?"

I have no idea and decide to take a wild guess. "Umm, is it when you hit the ball over the net?"

The eighth graders giggle.

"Before you interrupted me with your conversation with Miss Hopkins, I was telling the team that a volley is a shot you hit from the line that is closest to the net," says the coach. "All right, let me have you stand at the net and practice some volleys with Miss Clark over here."

I blush and get in place, and Mackenzie takes a place across from me on the other side of the net.

"All right. You two can work together until the end of practice," says the coach. "You girls go to court three," he points to Chloe and Mariama.

Just great. I wanted to be with my besties, and now I'm stuck with Big Mac.

My Granny Washington says, "If life hands you lemons, try to make lemonade," so I decide to make the best of things.

"Want to learn a secret handshake I made up?" I ask Mackenzie. "We can use it to get pumped up before our games. Let me show it to you."

I clasp Mackenzie's hand and shake it, then I stack my right fist on top of hers and put her left fist on mine. Next, I snap my fingers, give Mackenzie a hip bump, and put my hand out for another handshake.

"It's cute, right?" I look to her for approval.

Mackenzie holds her hands like a limp noodle and shrugs her shoulders. "I'm not into hand-shakes," she says.

"Oh, okay, sorry," I say. "Have you played tennis long?"

"Not too long," says Mackenzie. "My parents had me take lessons last summer."

"Me too," I say. "I went to a tennis camp at the YMCA."

"Great, let's start playing," says Mackenzie, stopping the conversation.

She grabs some balls from the bucket on the edge of the court and walks over to the other side.

We hit volleys back and forth for the next five minutes without speaking.

"She's actually not bad at tennis," I think.

"Good one, Mackenzie!" I say after she hits a fast, low ball that passes me.

"Thanks," she answers and doesn't say anything else.

My friends laugh and chatter away on the court beside us. I wish I could play triples with them and leave Big Mac alone.

Mackenzie returns another ball that I almost got past her. "Great job!" I say. "Wait, where are you going?"

Suddenly, she throws down her racket and sprints to the tennis court gates.

"I have to use the restroom," she says over her shoulder. "Be right back."

"But… what about the rest of our game?" I'm not sure what to do, so I sit on the bench in the center of the court.

Coach Quackenbush went inside to the gym a few minutes ago to get a cooler of water for us, so he doesn't see what's happening.

"Everything all right, Sophie?" asks Chloe from the other court.

"I guess, so," I answer. "Mackenzie just ran to the restroom." I bounce a ball on my racket for the next seven minutes until she returns.

When Mackenzie gets back, she picks up her racket like nothing happened.

"Ready to play?"

"Umm, sure," I say.

Coach Quackenbush returns and starts us on volley and baseline drills, where we hit the balls first from the back line on the court and then run to the line near the net to hit a short ball. We line up behind a cool-looking ball machine that makes a popping, suction cup sound as tennis balls swoosh out.

"Take that!" says Kennedy as she slams the ball over the net on her turn.

"Wow, she's got skills!" says Mariama.

"Too bad she acts likes Sharpay from *High School Musical*," whispers Chloe.

A few minutes later, Mackenzie gets her thermos from the edge of the court and starts guzzling water. No wonder she has to use the restroom so much. Sweat shows under the arms of her shirt, and her face drips.

"Is Mackenzie all right?" Chloe points and whispers to me. We're all hot, but she looks like she's about to faint. Coach walks over and gives Mackenzie a cool cloth to wipe her face with, and after sitting down for a couple minutes, she comes back to the group.

"I love your bracelet, Mackenzie." I admire the rose gold piece of jewelry on her wrist.

"Yeah, that's super cute. The flower charm is so pretty," says Chloe.

"Thanks," Mackenzie says. She covers the bracelet with her free hand and moves past us. Chloe glances at me, and we both shrug. So much for being friendly. It's funny Mackenzie is wearing such a nice bracelet, looking at her stretched out, stained, gray tee shirt and Xavier P.E. shorts.

Next, Coach has us playing practice points against each other.

"Gotcha!" I laugh as I hit a fast ball that gets past both Chloe and Mariama.

"Dang, Sophie, take it easy on a sister!" Chloe says with a laugh.

There must be at least three hundred tennis balls laying around the court by the time we get to the end of tryouts, but Coach shows us how to scoop them up in no time by placing several balls on the face of our tennis rackets and dumping them into the buckets he brought out. After we take a water break, he gathers us around, clipboard in hand.

"All right, you girls are looking good out here," he says. Based on what I've been seeing today I'm making the following roster. My eighth-grade girls, Kennedy, Lindsey, and Jackie are going to be playing first, second, and third singles, in that order, all right? All right. I want Chloe and Mariama and Sophie and Mackenzie as doubles partners.

"All right. I mean, okay, Coach," says Mariama.

"So we all made the team?!" asks Chloe.

"That's right," says the Coach.

The other girls high-five and fist bump. Mackenzie and I barely look at each other. I don't say anything when my friends start chattering because I'm so disappointed I might cry. It's good I made the team, but I can't believe Coach matched me with Mackenzie Clark!

Why can't she play singles? Then she'd be by herself. She doesn't want to talk to anybody so that would be right up her alley.

With Mackenzie as a partner, tennis won't even be fun. We have absolutely, positively, nothing in common. She barely speaks while I get in trouble at least once a week for talking in class. I'm on the top of the pyramid on the cheerleader squad; she sits in the bleachers. And to make things worse, Mackenzie doesn't even know how fun it is to have your own secret handshake! I'm not saying I could never be friends with her, but we are a complete mismatch. I don't see how this is going to work.

Chapter 3

Venus and Serena

My parents seem as excited about me making the tennis team as they were when I won the school spelling bee.

"Awesome sauce!" says Dad. "Venus and Serena were around your age when they got serious about their tennis training."

"Sports Shop is having a sale. Maybe we can get you some tennis outfits," says Mom.

"Nobody says 'awesome sauce,' Dad," I answer. "And I'm not that good at tennis. Everybody who tried out made the team."

"Well, we're still proud of you," says my mother. She turns to put a clean coffee mug up in the kitchen cabinet. "Playing on your first real sports team is an accomplishment."

We've had a late dinner, and the sweet scent of the hot peach cobbler Mom heated up for dessert still lingers in the air. My mother has just finished washing the dishes and is wiping off the counters while my eight-year-old brother, Cole, and I put our plastic cups and plates away. While we work, Dad sips on a cup of coffee and scrolls through his phone to check the list of patients who will be coming to get their teeth cleaned at his dental office on Monday.

"Who are Venus and Serena?" asks Cole. "Greek gods?"

"Only two of the best female tennis players in history," says Dad. "Both of them have won all the major tennis tournaments, like the French Open, the U.S. Open and Wimbledon."

"Even I know that," I say, rolling my eyes at my brother.

"Well, you won't be in any famous tournaments, Sophie," says Cole with a smirk. "You can't even win at the YMCA."

His dig reminds me of the time I played YMCA basketball in fourth grade and mistakenly made two baskets for the other team. How was I to know you're supposed to shoot on the opposite goal after halftime? Everybody on the team was mad at me because we ended up losing that game by four points.

"You take that back, Meanie!" I pinch Cole on his waist.

"Owww! You're hurting me!" he cries.

Eyes glued to his phone, Dad tunes us out. Mom doesn't notice our fighting either and reaches to put a platter in the cabinet.

When Cole tries to grab one of my braids, I move away, and then I pick up an empty milk carton to hit him on his boxy afro.

The racket startles my mother, and she nearly drops the glass platter.

"Enough with this violence! Sophie Washington, up to your room," she says, whirling around just in time to catch me in the act.

"No fair! Did you hear what Cole just said?"

"I saw what you just did and that's enough," she says. "There are better ways to handle an argument than beating each other up."

I trudge up the stairs and shut the door to my room with force, though I have enough sense not to slam it. I'd probably lose my cell phone. My parents have zero tolerance for tantrums.

"Come here, Poochie." My stomping sneakers wake up our Portuguese Water Dog, Bertram, from his nap, and he rolls on his back for a belly rub. I plop down on the edge of my double bed, and reach down to absently scratch his stomach's curly black fur.

Cole really gets on my nerves, I think, *always making fun of me. I'd pinch him again if he talked smack. How dare he say I won't win at tennis! I can beat him with my eyes closed.*

I'm still mad as I flip through the journal book Mom bought me to write my feelings in. The hot pink diary has a black glittery letter "S" on the cover for my name, Sophie Washington, and there is a key on a ribbon attached to lock it. The pages are blank because I don't want to mess up the pretty white paper with my not-so-neat handwriting, but I'm so upset right now I think I'll write my first entry. I'm not sorry I got in trouble for pinching Cole for his teasing, but deep down, I wonder if he's right.

Dear Diary,

I'm happy I made the tennis team with Chloe and Mariama, but I'm sad Mackenzie Clark is my partner. My dad wants me to be a really great tennis player like Venus or Serena Williams. With a partner like Mackenzie, I don't see how that will happen. She hardly talks to me; she didn't like the secret handshake I made up, and she ran off the court when we were practicing. I hope things go better at our practice next week because I just started playing tennis and I'm already ready to quit.

Chapter 4

Big Mac

"Hola! How were tennis tryouts?"

Valentina Martinez joins me, Chloe, and Mariama at our table during lunch. The sunny yellow socks she's wearing perfectly fit her cheerful personality, though they don't match our red and navy blue school uniforms. I glare at the black medical boot strapped on her foot with Velcro like it's my enemy. Why did Valentina have to get hurt? If she had tried out our coach probably would have matched me with her. Now I'm stuck with "Big Mac" as a partner.

Mackenzie still didn't speak to me after Coach Quackenbush announced us as partners. She just hefted up her backpack when we finished doing laps around the court and went to the carpool line. No goodbye, no see you later. Nothing.

I want to ask if I can get a new doubles partner as bad as the Cookie Monster wants a Chips Ahoy, but it seems like there's no other choice. I wouldn't want to stick my friends with Mackenzie, and the older girls are happy they're playing singles, so there's no way coach is moving them.

"Que pasa?" Valentina says and then crunches into her apple. "You have to tell me everything!"

When I first met Valentina earlier this year, I thought she was a phony because she sprinkles Spanish words in almost every conversation and likes to show off her gymnastics moves and get attention all the time. But after Valentina, her grandma, and her little brother, Hector, were forced to stay with me and my family when a hurricane hit our city, I realized she's a really nice person, and we became good friends. I can't imagine what school would be like without her. She's the captain of our cheerleading team and always keeps us laughing.

"Tennis is so much fun!" says Chloe. "I love all the cute outfits we get to wear. My mom is taking me and Mariama to the mall to buy some new skirts this weekend. There is this one mean eighth grader on our team named Kennedy, but she's playing singles, so we won't be around her much."

"Chloe and I are doubles partners, and we want all our practice outfits to match," says Mariama. "Want to come, too, Sophie? And even though you aren't on the team maybe you can join us, Valentina. We can all hang out at my house after."

"I have to check with my parents," I say.

"I'm in," says Valentina. "Just text me the time. Are you playing doubles, Sophie? Who's your partner?"

"Mackenzie Clark," I say, feeling like I have cotton in my mouth.

"You mean you're playing with 'Big Mac!?'" Toby Johnson, one of the best athletes in the sixth grade, plops his tray down at the table.

"Boy, put that back!" Chloe slaps his hand when Toby tries to steal one of her barbecue potato chips. After he switched to our school earlier this year, half the sixth-grade girls have a crush on Toby, me included. It seems as if he likes Chloe, and I think she likes him too, but they keep it hush hush.

"As much as she hates sports, I'm surprised that girl got on the tennis team," Toby says. "She always tried to get out of playing dodge ball in P.E. last year."

"Actually, she's not bad," I say. "My problem is that Mackenzie never speaks to me. Playing tennis with her is like being with a mime. She hardly speaks. It's as if she hates everyone."

"Something may be wrong with Mackenzie," says Nathan Jones, another boy in our grade. He slides into the last empty chair at our table and sets down his lunch tray.

"What do you mean?" I say.

"Remember when I hurt my leg last year and had to go to the nurse's office?" says Nathan, pushing his dark rimmed glasses up his nose. "She was crying when I came in. Nurse Bloomberg was giving her a shot, and I heard the nurse telling Mackenzie that she needs to make sure to take her medicine every day after lunch and to never miss it. Who gets shots every day?"

"No wonder she's so grouchy," says Chloe between bites of her peanut butter and jelly sandwich.

"What if it's something contagious?" I say. "Since I'm her partner I'll be near her every day at practice, so I might get it too."

"She can't be too bad off," says Mariama. "Think about it, if Makenzie was really that sick Xavier wouldn't let her come to school and she definitely wouldn't be able to play a sport."

"I guess you're right," I say. "I just feel bad because, until I got stuck with her, I was looking forward to playing tennis. This is going to be a long season."

Chapter 5

Practice Match

To get us ready for our upcoming match against our rival school, St. Regis, Coach Quackenbush has us play practice matches. Valentina's grandma has to work late and is picking her up at four-thirty this afternoon, and Toby and Nathan's track practice was cancelled because their coach is out of town, so they come to watch us.

"Do good for me guys!" says Valentina from the nearby mini bleachers. "Let's go! Vamanos!"

"All right, we've gone over the rules of tennis earlier today, so you know how to keep score," says Coach Quackenbush. He's wearing a whistle around his neck and carries his usual clipboard. "I want you to play each other, and the team that wins two out of three games will be declared the winner. Since we only have three singles players, I'll work with Kennedy while Lindsey and Jackie go against each other. All right. Let's see how we do, team!"

"All right!" we all parrot.

"Good luck in your matches, guys," Chloe says to the eighth-grade girls.

"We don't need luck unlike you little sixth graders," says Kennedy. "We have talent."

She and the older girls flounce off to their courts.

"Whatever," says Chloe with a roll of her eyes.

"They think they are 'all that' just because they were on the team last year," says Mariama. "I'd love to beat them in a game."

"Forget them," I say and pick up a can of new tennis balls Coach Quackenbush left on the court for us. "Come on, let's get going."

"Okay, let's get started," says Chloe. Her frilly red tennis skirt swings around her hips as she smacks the ball to us for the first serve. It bounces high in the air toward me.

"I got it!" I race forward.

"Mine!" Mackenzie comes over to my side of the court from the other direction. Surprised at her quick movement, I stumble.

Wham!

We run into each other. The ball bounces off my head, and I stagger to keep from falling.

"OMG! Sophie, are you all right?" Chloe and Mariama rush over to my side. I straighten up and blink to make the stars that are flashing in my eyes stop moving.

"Yeah, I'm okay."

I see the older girls on their courts putting their hands over their mouths to hide their giggles.

Now they'll make even more fun of me!

"I'm so sorry, Sophie!" says Mackenzie, her face apple-red.

"You're not supposed to hit the first ball unless you are receiving the serve," says Chloe. "Coach told us that when he was going over the rules."

"I'm sorry," Mackenzie says again with another blush. "I must have missed that."

I nod and stand still for a second to get my bearings, and then move back to my spot on the court. "I'm all right, let's keep playing."

"Should we call Coach over?" says Mariama. "He's bringing water out and didn't see what happened."

"Nah, I'm good," I say. The last thing I want is the coach to see me making a fool of myself. He won't think I'm ready to play singles when I ask to ditch Mackenzie as my partner.

"Whew! That was scary, Sophie," says Valentina. She talks across to us from outside the chain-link fence. "For a second I thought we might have to call el medico."

"We don't need the doctor." I stand. "Come on guys. I'm ready to play again."

"I didn't know there was tackling in tennis," says Toby with a laugh. "You all's games look rougher than football."

Chloe walks back to her place and serves the ball to me. I'm so flustered that this time I swing and miss. For some reason I feel a whole lot more nervous with my friends watching.

"MVP! MVP!" Nathan and Toby laugh and tease that I'm the most valuable player.

This is so embarrassing. I wish I could melt into the concrete like the Wicked Witch of the West from *The Wizard of Oz*.

Chapter 6

40-Love

Mackenzie and I get whopped by Mariama and Chloe, 40-Love, which in tennis terms means 40 to zero. I wonder why the inventors of tennis named a goose egg a word of affection. It should be 40-Nada, or 40-Zilch. I feel like I'm 40-Nothing as I wave goodbye to my friends and Mackenzie, pick up my backpack and racket and trudge to the parking area to wait for Mom. So far, playing tennis is the pits. The older girls are snobby, my partner doesn't talk to me, and now I'm becoming the team joke.

"You should have seen that ball bounce off Sophie's head!" I hear Nathan and Toby telling Carlton and Carly Gibson on the other end of the car pool area. "She's the team MVP!"

I turn my back and ignore them.

Thank goodness Valentina didn't have her cell phone out or the whole school would know. She loves to take selfies and other pictures with her phone camera and post them to social media. With my luck it would have gone viral.

"How was your day, sweetie?" asks my mother after she pulls up to get me.

"Just great," I answer.

It's a good thing Cole isn't in the car. The last thing I need to deal with is his teasing, or worse yet, listen to his lame jokes.

The one he had this morning was the worst.

"Where did tennis players go on their date? The Tennis Ball!"

"Where's Cole?" I ask my mother.

"Your father picked him up early to go to a Houston Rockets basketball game downtown," she says. "A doctor in his office building has season tickets and couldn't make it this evening, so it's just us girls."

"Yay!" I cheer.

Things are looking up. I love to have girl time with my mom. She takes me out to my favorite places to eat for burgers or pizza, and sometimes we watch a movie Dad and Cole can't stand, like the *Princess Diaries*. Of course, it's too late for us to hang out as we would on a weekend afternoon, but I'll settle for eating out. That'll be the perfect pick-me-up after that terrible tennis practice.

But Mom deflates my hopes quicker than a popped helium balloon.

"I've got some paperwork to do for the office, so we can heat up some of the leftover chili we had last night for dinner."

"Can't we go out since Dad and Cole are at the game?"

"I'm sorry to disappoint you, Sophie, but I really need to get my work finished," says Mom. "Maybe we can do something special this weekend, or next, just the two of us."

I nod my head and look out the window. I know I shouldn't be mad, but I am. Cole and Dad are having a boy's night out, and now that Mom and I have the chance to do something fun she doesn't want to.

"Oh, I forgot to ask you, Sophie, how was tennis practice?"

Why'd she have to ask me that? A tear slips from the corner of my eye, and I sniff to hold it in.

I don't want to answer because I know she'll be able to tell that something is wrong.

"Are you sniffling over there? What's going on?"

"Nothing. I just sneezed," I say.

"Uh huh." Mom glances at me as we sit at a red light.

Instead of turning down the road toward our house, she heads straight to a strip center filled with specialty shops.

"We don't have time to go out for a full meal, but how about we get a bit of ice cream for a treat?"

Mom pulls up to an ice cream parlor. "It's been awhile since just you and I had our own time after school without Cole around."

I try to smile, but I still don't feel great. I sit in the passenger side while Mom unsnaps her seatbelt.

"Why aren't you getting out, Sophie? Did something happen at tennis practice? What's going on?"

She pats her hand on my shoulder, and my eyes start to water.

"I'm the worst one on the team!" I say. "Even worse than Mackenzie. That's why coach made me and her partners!"

"Didn't you tell me that your friends are beginners? They can't be that much better than you."

"Well, they are! And I hate it! Mackenzie and I got beat 40-Love in our game, and Nathan and Toby are calling me the MVP!!"

"The MVP is a good thing, isn't it?"

"Not the way they are saying it. I'm a big fat joke!"

"Awwww, come here, Sweetie! I'm sorry you've had a bad day!" My mother slides over and gives me a hug. "Let's get our ice cream and talk about it. Maybe we can come up with a plan to help you improve."

I reluctantly follow Mom into the ice cream shop, and I must admit I do feel better when I see the bins of brightly-colored ice cream behind the counter and spot my favorite, Rocky Road. My mother and father are health nuts who don't let us eat a lot of junk food and sweets, so it's not too often that we get ice cream, especially on a school night.

"I want mine in a sugar cone, please," I say to the tall man with tattoos up and down his arms working at the counter. My mother orders a single scoop of butter pecan.

We sit at a back table with our cones, and Mom helps me come up with ways I can make things better on the team.

"I felt bad when Coach Quackenbush matched me up with Mackenzie. She's mean, she's clumsy, and she doesn't want to learn the secret partner handshake I made up. I'm not good at tennis either, so with her as my partner I'll probably lose all my games."

"It's not nice to call people names, Sophie. You need to have a positive attitude," says my mother. "You shouldn't be so hard on Mackenzie. She may have problems you don't know about. And you can work to improve your playing. Let's see if your dad can take you out to practice this weekend. He played tennis some in high school."

"That was in the 1900s!" I say. "Is he still good?"

"I think he might remember some tips from way back when," says my mother with a chuckle. "Give it a go with your father. Things just might

look up. Here, wipe your mouth." She hands me a napkin. "You've got chocolate on your face."

Talking to Mom made me feel a lot better, and the double scoop of ice cream didn't hurt either. By the time we head back to the car I'm smiling again. I didn't get forty points today like Chloe and Mariama, but I definitely got the love.

Chapter 7

Weekend Warrior

I've dotted all my "I's" and crossed all my "T's" when I set off to practice with my father on Saturday morning. Wheaties for breakfast? Check. Sun visor to block the glare when I'm hitting the ball? Check. New tennis shoes, and new tennis racket? Check, check.

Mom said she wasn't going to spend a lot of money on tennis gear until we saw if I really liked the sport, but there was a sale on outfits and rackets when she took Cole to Sports Shop this week for new socks, and she couldn't help herself. I got two new skirts with matching tops, a sun visor, and special sneakers.

I feel like an official tennis player, and almost as stylish as Chloe, as I swish around in my white tennis skirt. I bounce on my toes in "ready position," like Coach Quackenbush taught us in practice, while Dad sets down a large bucket of tennis balls on the opposite side of the court. I may not play like Venus and Serena yet, but I'm on my way.

"Let's see what you've got, sport," says Dad as he reaches in the bucket and gently tosses me a fuzzy yellow ball. There are probably one hundred tennis balls in there, all for me to hit. This is going to be a looong practice.

If Dad throws the balls directly to me, I do pretty well returning them, but I start swinging and missing again, when he changes things up.

"We need to work on your positioning during your swing," says Dad. "When you approach the ball to hit it, turn your body to the side, bend your knees and then swing through with your racket, like this. He shows me what to do, and I watch closely.

As the next ball comes toward me, I imitate the movements my father made, swing through with my racket, and the ball makes it over the net!

"Good job!" says Dad. We practice this move for about fifteen more minutes and I get into a rhythm with hitting the balls.

"Take a water break and then pick up the balls," says Dad.

"All of them?" I answer. "There're probably fifty or sixty balls out here!"

"Scoop them up on your racket and dump them into the bucket," says my father. "Let's get moving."

It takes me about five minutes to gather up the balls and then my father picks up the pace of my lesson, throwing the tennis balls from side to side

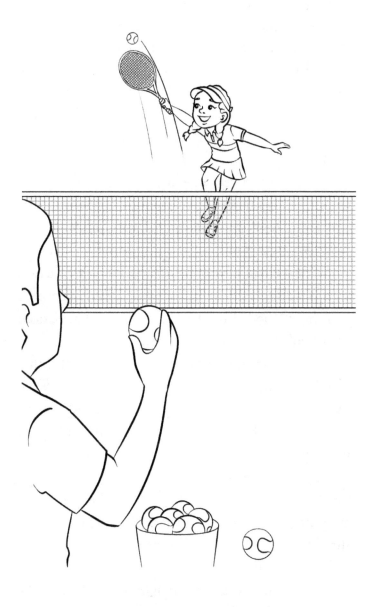

on the court for me to hit so I have to run really fast. I surprise myself by making it to most of them. I hit a few into the net, but I'm not doing half bad.

"Great practice!" says my father after more than an hour has gone by. "How do you feel?"

"Much better," I answer. "I can hit the higher balls over the net without missing now. Thanks, Dad."

"We'll practice some more tomorrow, and it would be good if you can hit some with your partner. There are strategies I can teach you as doubles partners to help you play better as a team."

"Mackenzie never talks to me during practice, so I'm not sure if she'll want to," I say. "Once he sees how good I'm getting I hope that Coach Quackenbush will let me play singles."

"A true winner knows how to work with other people, Sophie," says my father. "Your coach matched you and this girl Mackenzie together for a reason. You shouldn't be trying to bail on your partner."

"But…" I begin.

"I don't want you to be a quitter before you've even begun, Sophie," my father interrupts. "You should stick with your coach's plan for a while before giving up."

Dad puts his key in the ignition and starts the car to head home, and I turn my head toward the window to pout. My father doesn't notice because he takes an emergency phone call from one of his dental patients.

He just doesn't understand. Mackenzie doesn't want to be my partner. She barely even speaks to me. I thought tennis would be fun, but being matched with her is worse than being forced to do extra homework. I'm going to practice as hard as I can to get better, and then I'm asking Coach if I can play by myself.

Chapter 8

Chirp, Chirp

I'm still Buzz Lightyears away from being as good as the eighth graders, but I'm definitely better since my father started helping me.

"Nice volley, Sophie," says Coach Quackenbush, who shuffles around all the courts to observe. "I liked that spin."

I've just hit a hard, short, shot that landed right at Chloe's feet. Dad's been teaching me a way to hit the tennis ball called the "spin" that makes it bounce away from my opponents when it lands.

"Dang, Sophie, take it easy on us," says Mariama. "You nearly hit my arm."

"She hit the ball where she was supposed to, Miss Asante," says Coach, overhearing. "*You* need to move your feet."

"Yes, sir," says Mariama with a blush.

"Sor-ry," I mouth to my friend, but I'm smiling inside.

I am really learning how to play. Dad's been taking me out after I get home from school and on the weekends, so I've gotten private lessons for fourteen days straight, along with our regular team practice. After school practice has been more fun the past few days too because Mackenzie has been absent, so I don't have to deal with her ignoring me. I'm still mad that she wouldn't learn my secret tennis handshake. I was looking forward to doing that with my partner.

"Just make sure Sophie's keeping up with her school work," my mother tells my father after we come in that evening. "You act like you really do want her to go pro."

"I'm just happy to see Sophie getting excited about a team sport," says my father. "She's never taken much interest in athletics before."

"I want to learn to play tennis, too," whines Cole. "You are always teaching Sophie, but you don't teach me anything, Dad."

"Now you know that's not true, son," says my father. "You and I play basketball together at the gym and outside on your goal all the time. And who taught you to tie your shoes and to do your times tables? I'm trying to help your sister become more competitive at tennis since she's enjoying playing."

"Sophie has also been slacking on her chores since you two have started on this tennis kick," says Mom before setting a mug on the table. "Cole set the table himself all last week."

That is so not true, but I don't say anything because I don't want to get into trouble for being sassy. Half the time when we're getting things set up for dinner, Cole is wrestling with Bertram or sneaking to play his handheld video game. When it's our week to do the dishes, he goofs around with the suds, and I end up cleaning everything myself to keep from hearing Mom fuss. It's about time my brother had to do some work around here.

The grumbling of my stomach interrupts my thoughts. Tonight, Mom's making steaks for dinner, and the smoky, char-grilled smell fills the kitchen when she brings a few in from the smoker out back.

Mmmm, mmmm, mmmm...Bertram starts begging as soon as Mom carries the platter of sizzling steaks to the stove.

"Let's go outside, Poochie." She steers him by his curly black fur toward the backyard. He looks up at her with Beanie Baby eyes, and she pats his head.

"You know I hate to do it, but out you go. We want to eat in peace."

Bertram is the king of dinnertime begging. Mom's been trying to train him to sit still when we eat, but Cole and I keep sneaking and giving him bites of food, so it hasn't been working.

It's hard to believe that my mother was against us getting a pet last year. She never wanted us to have one until Bertram followed me and Cole

home, and we found out that his fur doesn't shed so she doesn't sneeze or get itchy with her allergies around him. Though one of his favorite past times is chewing up shoes, our parents let us keep Bertram. Now he's like one of the family. Mom buys Bertram treats and takes him to the groomer so much that sometimes I think she likes him better than me or Cole.

"I guess old boy likes steak, salad, and baked potatoes, just like the rest of us," says Dad, watching Bertram whimper at the back door.

"He can have my salad," says Cole, scooping butter and sour cream on his potato.

"Not so much sour cream, young man," says Mom. "and forget about giving your salad to the dog. You need all the veggies you can get."

"What's your coach say about how you're playing, Sophie?" says Dad.

"He says I'm really improving," I say between bites of steak. "Coach Quackenbush doesn't know that I've been doing extra work with you, so he thinks he's the best coach ever. Mariama and Chloe get mad 'cause he walks around more with his clipboard than he teaches us anything."

Chirp, chirp, chirp.

Sparrow-like peeps sound from the family room.

"What's that noise?" asks Mom, noticing it too.

"I think it's coming from the fireplace," says Dad.

There's a fluttering, and the squeaking stops when we get quiet.

"It's a bird!" exclaims Cole.

Chapter 9

Alvinn!!

"Cole, get my flashlight." My father slides his chair from the kitchen table to investigate.

"Please don't tell me there's another animal in here!" says Mom.

"We need to evacuate!" I say. I jump up and grab my tennis racket from the corner, ready to attack anything Dad might find.

Our parents sometimes joke that living in our neighborhood, which is located in the Houston suburbs, is like starring on a reality show on the *Animal Planet* channel because we're always seeing wild animals. Last year, we ran across an eight-foot-alligator in a stream not far from where we live when we were out on a family bike ride, and a raccoon somehow chewed his way into our attic a few months ago.

"Here, Dad! Let's see what it is!!" Cole bounds to my father with his mega-watt flashlight.

I back into the kitchen as far away from the family room action as I can get, still holding out my tennis racket.

"Put that thing down, Sophie," says Mom.

All these wildlife encounters get Cole excited, but me, not so much. The only animals I want to be around are my goldfish Goldy, and our dog Bertram, or maybe a monkey behind bars in a zoo. I do *not* want a Tweety bird flying around our house.

My father shines the light into the fireplace grate, and my mother stands beside him.

"Stay back, Cole," she says and holds her arms out.

"I see a head!" my brother shouts as they peer through the black mesh screen, and I shudder.

"What in the world is that?" says Mom.

Dad flashes his light in the grate again and looks more carefully.

"It's some kind of rodent!" he says.

"We have rats?!!" I shriek.

There is more rustling in the fireplace.

"The thing that's moving has a bushy tail." says Cole as he peers through the screen.

"Oh no!" I say. "They are going to get us."

"Don't worry, Sophie," my father says with a chuckle. "I think it's a family of squirrels. A rat wouldn't have a tail like that. It was colder than usual outside last week, and I guess they got in our fireplace somehow and had babies."

"There's three baby squirrels!" says Cole with excitement. He shines the flashlight higher up in the fireplace. "See them wiggling? Look at their little heads!"

"Careful, Cole," says my mother.

A shadow of a small busy tail flashes behind the screen.

"Ewww!" I exclaim.

This is just great. Alvin and the Chipmunks have moved into our family room! How are we going to sleep tonight? Where can we finish dinner? I look at the chopped-up pieces of steak getting cold on my plate. No way am I going to be able to eat with those critters so close by.

"We have to get the squirrels out of here," says my father. "Do we have a cardboard box?"

"Don't open up the fireplace!" says Mom. "Those things might get loose in the house. We'd better call pest control."

"It's too late for them to come out this evening," says Dad. "It's after business hours."

"They're cute," says Cole. "See the straw from their nest?"

"I wonder how they got in here?" says Dad. "The chimney is closed. Maybe they found an opening in the attic."

"I thought they sealed it up when we they got that raccoon up there," says Mom.

"Squirrels will chew through anything," Dad answers.

"This is *so* not funny!" I say. "Please don't open the fireplace, Dad. What if they hurt you? They could have rabies."

"They aren't going to hurt me, Sweetie. Calm down." He goes out to the garage and comes back with thick gloves on his hands and a shoebox.

"Hey, Dad, that's the box my Jordan tennis shoes came in," says Cole. "I was saving that."

"Shut up, Cole!" I say in irritation.

"Sophie Washington, watch your language!" says Mom.

I pick up my tennis racket again and stand in ready position. If a squirrel runs out of that fireplace, I'm going to swing this thing like I've never swung before!

Things get quiet in the fireplace, so I'm guessing the mother squirrel ran off when she heard us arguing and saw the bright flashlight. Hopefully, it blinded her.

"Be careful, Daddy!" I close my eyes while he opens the grate.

"Thank goodness we haven't started a fire in there lately," says my mother.

"Wonder what roasted squirrel smells like?" says Cole.

Squeak. Squeak. Squeak.

"Look, Sophie! Look!" shouts Cole.

I peek open one eye to see my father pulling three baby squirrels out of the fireplace, one by one, and placing them in the old shoebox. They have pink bellies and grayish colored backs, and their eyes are sealed shut.

"Get them out of here, Dad!" I say with a cringe.

"Leave the box in the garage and I'll call pest control in the morning," says Mom.

Squeak, squeak, squeak, squeal the baby squirrels again.

My father clears the straw and grass from the animals' nest and seals up the now-quiet fireplace.

I won't be able to sleep tonight knowing that a mama squirrel could still be running around our house. Cole thinks it's hilarious when I tell him the squirrels remind me of Alvin and the Chipmunks.

"Allvinn!" he yells.

"Why can't Sophie and a squirrel be friends?" My brother makes up another of his silly jokes. "Because the squirrel would drive her nuts!"

"Now that's enough, kids, go on upstairs for your baths and I'll clean up the kitchen tonight," says Mom. She pulls out a can of Lysol disinfectant and sprays around the fireplace grate.

"You never can be too sure about germs."

I thought I'd have nightmares, but I start drifting off to sleep not long after Dad tucks me in. All the excitement with tennis and the squirrels has worn me out. Tomorrow we have practice matches to get ready for our first real tennis tournament

next week. Coach Quackenbush said he may be making some changes in the lineups based on how we do. This could be my chance to ditch Mackenzie, and I can't wait.

Chapter 10

Mean Girl

On the way home from school Cole rattles on about a special art show Xavier's having for the lower school kids.

"We're going to copy paintings of famous artists like Pablo Picasso, and one painter who cut his ear off, I forget his name…Vinny Go?"

"I believe it's Vincent Van Gogh," says Mom.

"Yeah, that's it!" says Cole. "We're writing papers about their lives, and our teacher is hanging them on the wall. There'll be a special art day at school, Mom, when you and Dad can come see all the paintings and get cookies and punch."

"That sounds very nice, Cole. I'll be looking forward to it," says my mother.

I've always thought of art as a class to take for an easy A or B with no homework, but Cole is really into it. He's great at drawing, and a picture he drew that shows a Texas Longhorn in a field of bluebonnet flowers won a ribbon at the Houston Livestock and Rodeo last year.

I usually tell Mom all about my day during our commute, too, but I don't think she'll be too happy to hear what happened at tennis practice this afternoon, so I stay quiet.

"Hey, listen, Sophie, I have some funny new tennis jokes." Cole pulls out a joke book my grandma sent him that he keeps in the back seat.

"Which state has the most tennis players? Tennis-ee."

"Why is tennis a noisy game? Because each player raises a racket!"

"Those jokes are so corny, Cole. Mom, please make him stop!"

As soon as we pull into the garage, I look over to see whether the shoebox with the baby squirrels is still around. My Dad left them in the garage overnight so that they'd be safe, and my mother was supposed to be calling pest control to get them this morning. All day at school, I've been scared she'd forget and they would get loose somehow.

I don't see the box anymore, so I figure it's safe to ask about our unwelcome visitors.

"Hey, Mom, did they get the squirrels?"

"Yes, thank goodness, the man from pest control came this morning and took them. Unfortunately, he says the poor things probably won't survive because their mother most likely won't take them back. He took them with him to set them free in the woods, but said another animal will probably eat them. He also sealed up the areas on the roof where the mother squirrel got in the chimney and left a trap in the attic. He thinks she is gone now, but the trap will get her if she's still in the attic and comes out."

"That's sad," I say. "I don't want anything bad to happen to the baby squirrels. I just don't want them in our house."

"I know what you mean, Sophie," says Mom. "Sometimes weaker creatures just can't make it."

I think about what Nathan said about something being wrong with Mackenzie. She acts like she doesn't care about anything, but maybe she's somehow a weaker creature too. Coach still hasn't told us why she's missed so many days of practice, and none of the girls has asked him.

After we drop off our book bags in the kitchen, I rush to my room to grab my journal. A lot went on at tennis practice today, and I have some feelings to sort out.

Dear Diary,

I was so happy at practice, but by the time I left, I felt terrible. Since Mackenzie hasn't been coming to tennis, I thought maybe she quit the team. I was talking about it with Kennedy and my friends, and I'm not sure, but I think I heard her crying in the girls' locker room afterward. I said mean things about Mackenzie to make Kennedy like me. When we went into practice, I saw her run across the soccer fields from the woods, but I didn't tell anyone, not even Chloe or Mariama. I wonder if she's been hiding out there all week instead of going to practice? I'm not sure if I should tell somebody or ask Mackenzie about it at school tomorrow. She got in her mom's car when we were in the pickup line, so I know she's not lost in the woods. It's funny that we've been on the same team for almost three weeks and I haven't really spoken to her.

"Where's your partner, 'Big Mac,' been, Sophie?" Kennedy came up to me and my friends while we were changing for tennis in the locker room. "Probably off somewhere eating a Happy Meal."

"Or maybe in the bathroom," I said. "She goes there all the time."

"Maybe if she keeps skipping practice you can get a real partner," said Kennedy.

"That's a good one," I said as I watched her walk off.

My friends shook their heads.

"That girl is so mean," said Mariama. "It's a good thing Mackenzie wasn't here to hear her."

"Yeah, I can't believe you were going along with Kennedy, Sophie," Chloe said.

"I just said she was funny," I answered. "And it's not like Mackenzie is going to win anyone's friendly neighbor award. She barely even answers me when I speak to her."

"You heard what Nathan said about her having to get shots," said Chloe. "For all we know she could be in the hospital."

"Okay, okay, maybe I shouldn't have laughed at Kennedy's joke," I said as we neared the door. "Mackenzie hasn't really said anything out and out mean to me, I just feel bad that she doesn't talk."

When I came back in the locker room to get the notebook I left, I thought I heard someone crying. After I saw Mackenzie run across the field later, I realized it must have been her.

"Hey, isn't that your tennis partner?" Chloe asked and pointed when we saw a flash of short black hair enter the gray minivan that pulled up in the pickup lane.

"That sure looks like her," said Mariama. "Wonder why she hasn't been coming to practice?"

I didn't say anything.

Now I'm not sure what to do. I can't call Mackenzie tonight because I don't have her telephone number, but maybe I should apologize when I see her at school tomorrow. Everything was going my way, and I'd really forgotten about her until I saw Mackenzie cross the soccer field during practice. What if my mean words caused her to skip tennis? Even if she doesn't come back to the team, I wouldn't have a good time being someone else's partner, or even playing singles, knowing I ran her away. I have to find her tomorrow and make things right.

Chapter 11

The Real MVP

When I go by Mackenzie's locker the next morning, I find out she's absent from school again.

"I've been trying to get in touch with her, but she's not answering any of my calls or texts," says Liv Jones, one of her few friends in the school. "I think she said something about going to Austin with her Mom. Her parents both travel out-of-town a lot for their jobs, and she stays with her nanny most of the time unless they take her with them."

"Lucky," I say. "My family would never go on an out-of-town trip when it wasn't a school holiday."

"Yeah, Kenzie's out a lot," says Liv.

Like Mackenzie, Liv is really pale. Her hair is a dark red color, and she likes to wear multicolored striped socks with her school uniform.

"Could you give her my number and have her call me?" I say and hold out my cell phone. "I have to talk with her about something going on, on the tennis team."

"Sure," says Liv. "I'll punch your number in my phone."

I doubt Mackenzie will really call, but I feel better knowing that I did do something. I'm too chicken to take her number.

If I didn't feel bad about Mackenzie, today's practice would be perfect. I play with Lindsey against Kennedy and Jacqueline, and our game is great.

"You got this, MVP!" cheers Valentina from the stands. She's been coming to nearly all our practices and does her homework while she waits for her grandma to pick her up. "You guys are going to do great."

Kennedy rolls her eyes.

My heart beats fast as she and Jacqueline walk to the center court. Kennedy wears an expensive looking pink and purple tennis outfit and carries a floral athletic bag with a pouch on the side. She unzips it and pulls out her tennis racket.

"Ooooo, fancy," I say in admiration. "Where did you get that bag?"

"At a store for real MVPs," she says.

"Aww, snap!" says Jacqueline.

"Who cares?" I say. "Let's play."

"M or W?" Kennedy says and points to the "W" Wilson brand symbol on the face of her tennis racket.

"W, for Washington," I say.

Kennedy twirls her racket to see which side the tennis racket face lands on, which lets us know who serves first. Being the first to serve is an advantage in tennis if you can control where you hit the ball.

The spin lands on M, and Kennedy shakes her shoulder length braids happily.

"Our serve. I'll serve first, Jacqueline," she says.

I hold my breath as I stand at the back, or baseline, of the tennis court, to receive Kennedy's serve, and she hits the ball to me in the middle of the serving box. Bending my knees like Dad taught me, I swing, and hit the ball back over the net. *Got it!*

I start to breathe again as I hit Jacqueline's return. The ball lands right on the baseline, and I'm able to smash it between Kennedy and Jacqueline with my special spin shot to win the point.

"Great job, Sophie," says Lindsey.

Kennedy and Jacqueline seem surprised that I do so well.

"Not bad for a little sixth grader," says Kennedy after we win a game during my serve.

"Thank you, Granny," I say with a laugh, and Kennedy actually gives me a fist bump.

"Lindsey, Sophie, I need to talk to you, all right" Coach Quackenbush calls us over after we finish. "Since Mackenzie has been missing so many practices, I'm thinking about changing the line-up and matching you two together as the second doubles team. We'll have to forfeit the number three singles game, but I think this is our best bet to get enough points to win the match."

"I wanted to play singles, but that will be fine with me, Coach," says Lindsey. "Sophie and I had a fun game today."

"Yeah, I agree," I say with a smile.

"You did good for a sixth grader," says Kennedy.

"Good game, kid," says Jacqueline.

For the first time since I joined the tennis team, I feel like I really belong.

Chapter 12

Assembly

We have a middle school assembly this morning, so our first period class is cancelled. I walk by Mackenzie's locker on my way to the assembly hall to talk to her, but she's not there.

"Hey, Sophie, how's it going?" says Rani Patel, an Indian girl in our grade who was a member of a computer coding team, called Code One, with me, Chloe, Valentina, and Mariama, earlier this year. "Long time, no see."

"I've missed hanging out with you, Rani, now that the coding competition is over."

"It was a lot of fun, wasn't it? Maybe we can join up again next year. How's your little brother, Cole?"

"Still as corny as ever," I say. "He wanted me to tell you he got a new joke book."

Rani is one of the few girls that my little brother doesn't think is "yucky." They met when she came over our house once to work on the coding project, and he was over the moon when he found out she likes silly jokes as much as he does.

"On your way to the assembly?" asks Rani.

"Yeah, I heard about it in homeroom. What's it about?" I ask.

"Dunno," says Rani. "Something about healthy eating."

"Sounds like loads of fun," I groan.

"Well, at least we miss first period," says Rani with a swing of her long, black ponytail. "I was dreading science class because we were going to dissect frogs today."

"We did that earlier in the year, and it was gross," I agree. "Want to sit over here?"

Sixth through eighth graders fill up the auditorium, and Rani and I take a seat near the center of the room with other members of our grade.

"Hey, Sophie and Rani!" Chloe, Valentina, and Mariama wave at us from five rows up.

"Hi!" we wave back.

My heart beat quickens when I see the back of Mackenzie's head a couple of rows in front of us. *She finally made it to school!* She's sitting next to her friend Liv. I guess she didn't want to call me during the time she was absent. I wonder if she'll show up at tennis practice today?

"Good morning, students, and welcome," says our principal, Mr. Jenkins. "As part of our science unit on healthy living, Dr. Avril Wright, a local nutritionist, is here with us this morning to talk about foods that are good for your body."

I slump down in my seat. It's bad enough that my parents are health nuts who think baked eggplant fries are a treat, now they're getting on the veggie train at school.

Wearing a loose floral skirt, a light yellow, flowy blouse, at least twenty jangly bracelets, and Jesus sandals, Dr. Wright reminds me of a hippie from the 1970s.

"Great to see you kids. How many of you are excited about fresh foods, like broccoli, green beans, and kale?"

No one raises their hands.

"That's about what I thought," Dr. Wright says with a laugh and runs her hands through her frizzy blonde hair. "How many of you like to eat snack food?"

Most of the kids in the room, except those who are sneaking to play games on their phones or sleeping, put an arm in the air.

"Now that's more like it!" Dr. Wright says enthusiastically. "Did you know that healthy eating and flavorful, fun, eating can be one and the same? It just takes having some knowledge about ways to prepare foods that nourish and sustain you while giving you all the yummy tastes and feels. Okay, who in here knows how to cook?"

Five or six out of the hundreds of kids in the auditorium raise their hands.

"That's all?" Dr. Wright looks around the room in surprise. "Looks like your parents need to be doing some work when it comes to life skill training. All right, today I'm going to teach you kids how to make at least three healthy and flavor-filled snacks that you can enjoy after school every day. These snacks will not only fill you up and taste delicious, but they'll also provide vitamins and nutrients that your body needs to grow in a healthy way. Don't worry if you're not chosen to volunteer or you haven't learned to do food prep yet. I'm going to leave your principal with copies of recipes of all the easy to make snacks we're preparing today so you can try them on your own. Are we ready, guys? Let's go!"

Dr. Wright chooses an eighth-grade boy named Timmy, and Kennedy from my tennis team, a girl named Jennifer, and a boy named Hakim from seventh grade, and the Gibson twins, Carly and Carlton, from our grade, to join her on the stage.

"I'll have my three volunteer teams each make a different snack. Team One will prepare a Green Apple Cinnamon Smoothie, Team Two can make Banana Dog Bites, and Team Three can prepare Guacamole and chips."

Dr. Wright leads the three groups to tables set up on the center of the stage. Each table includes food and prepping materials. The finished product is also displayed, I guess so we can see what the snacks are really supposed to look like in case the groups mess them up.

"Okay, the recipes and the ingredients for all these wonderful snacks are right here on the table. After you finish making them, I'd like each group to eat a sample and share how you like them with your classmates in the audience."

"That apple smoothie looks gross," says Rani.

"I know," I say. "I don't like to eat or drink anything green."

The volunteers read through their recipes and begin work.

"This is like a live version of one of those reality TV cooking shows," I say.

Kennedy and Timmy finish up their snack first. I guess it's easiest since they just had to mix some things up in the blender to make the smoothie. Dr. Avril walks over to them with her microphone.

"How do you like it?"

"Not bad," says Timmy, taking a sip.

"It's all right, but I really don't like green apples that much, so it's not my favorite," says Kennedy. She hands the microphone back to Dr. Wright, who makes her way to the second group that is just finishing up. Before she reaches them, there's a commotion in the audience, and a girl shouts, "Help! My friend just passed out!"

The students in the row in front of us stand, so my view is blocked. But I can see who screamed out from the audience, it's Mackenzie's friend Liv!

Chapter 13

Big Mac Attack

"Clear the aisle, children. Get back in your seats!" Mr. Jenkins presses through the crush of kids to see what the problem is.

"Someone, call security and the school nurse."

There's a hush in the auditorium as kids crane their necks for a better view.

In the rows ahead of us I see Chloe, Valentina, and Mariama standing on tiptoes to get a glimpse. Valentina pulls out her cell phone, holds it high in the air, and starts clicking. She's constantly snapping photos and says she wants to be a photographer when she grows up.

A girl with short, bluish-black hair is lying on two chairs.

"It's my tennis partner!" I say, when the crowd parts for the nurse.

"Whoa! Big Mack just had an attack," says a brown curly-haired boy beside me named Jacob Greer.

Nurse Bloomberg looks at Mackenzie's bracelet,

and then says something to the security guards. They ease Mackenzie on a stretcher, lift her up, and move her out of the auditorium.

"What's going on?" says Rani.

"I saw a little of her face," I say. "She wasn't talking. I think she's unconscious."

The nurse comes back to Mr. Jenkins and they talk for about five minutes while my classmates and I try to solve the mystery.

"Hey, Liv, what were you and Mackenzie talking about before she fell? Did she look green or anything?" Jacob asks.

"Nothing really," says Liv. "She just suddenly started fanning herself with her homeroom folder, saying it was hot, and the next thing I knew she was falling on the floor."

'She's missed tennis practice since the end of last week," I tell Rani. "I thought it was because she didn't like it, and also because she overheard some people talking about her, but maybe she was sick."

"This is so strange," says Rani.

"Attention, everyone." Mr. Jenkins is back on the stage and taps his finger on the microphone. "One of your classmates had a non-emergency 'episode,' that doesn't appear to be serious. No need to worry, she should be fine and able to return to class this afternoon or tomorrow. However, due to the time taken by this incident, our assembly is concluded. I'd like rows one through five to line up and file out."

I pick up my backpack and stand up by my seat.

"Ah, man! Why couldn't we have had an emergency during my math test today?!" says Jacob. "My favorite show was on TV last night and I didn't study. I was hoping this assembly would run through second period."

"Do you believe that nothing serious happened to your tennis partner?" asks Rani.

"Uh, uh," I say. "This is just too weird. She hasn't been at practice all week, and Nathan Jones said he saw the nurse telling her she needs shots every day for some sickness she has. There's something they aren't telling us."

Dr. Wright picks up the microphone from the stand. "So sorry to see your classmate become ill. But I'm glad to hear the good news that whatever is going on is not serious. I will leave copies of the snack recipes with your principal so they can be distributed to you in the next few days. I'll be checking back in with him to see how you like them. My personal favorites are the Banana Dog Bites."

I roll my eyes. Who cares about eating good-for-you snacks at a time like this? I want some answers. What made Mackenzie pass out? And why's she been skipping tennis practice? I saw a show on the news where a kid around my age got a disease called cancer and died. Could Mackenzie have something like that? I've got to figure out what is wrong with her! I'm going to camp out at her locker at the end of school today to find out what's up.

Chapter 14

Sugar

Mackenzie doesn't show up at her locker after school, but I'm in luck the next morning. Though the hallway is crammed with kids in school uniforms rushing to their lockers, she's easy to spot. The fluorescent school lighting gives her black, dyed hair an unnatural purplish tint that makes her stand out in the crowd. I'm surprised the school lets her keep it because being a private school, Xavier has a strict dress code. They made one boy in my grade get a haircut last week after he let the sides grow down to his chin.

I've been looking for Mackenzie for days, but now that I have the chance to apologize, I'm not sure how to go about it. What if she yells at me in front of everyone or refuses to talk to me at all? My father says the best way to take off a Band Aid, or handle something scary, is to rip it off, or do it quickly, so I boldly walk up to her.

"Hey, Mackenzie, where have you been? Are you okay? I saw what happened at the assembly yesterday, and you haven't been to practice."

"I'm sure you were as happy as a 'Happy Meal,' that I've been gone," she says, frowning at me. "I saw you playing with Kennedy and the eighth graders when I skipped practice, and you didn't seem to miss me too much. In fact, you were laughing and prancing around like you were having the time of your life!"

"I don't eat Happy Meals," I answer. "Look, Mackenzie, I'm sorry if I said or did anything to hurt your feelings. I know you probably heard me the other day, and I don't want to run you off the tennis team. I was just upset that you hardly talked to me at practice and acted like you didn't want to be my partner."

"You're right, I don't want to be your partner," says Mackenzie. "I don't want to play tennis at all. Coach Quackenbush probably didn't want me to try out either. My parents begged him to put me on the team after my doctor and the school nurse said I need to have more exercise to 'help manage my sugar.'"

"Sugar? What's that mean?" I ask.

"Don't try to be funny!" says Mackenzie. She points her finger at me. "I heard you laughing about me with Kennedy."

"All right, I was laughing, but I was just mad at you for not talking to me at practice. What's going on?"

"Who would want to talk to somebody like you?" says Mackenzie. "You pretend you're sweet little Sophie Washington, everybody's best friend, but you're no better than Kennedy. You're fake, and you're phony, and I wish I'd never been matched as your partner!"

"What!??" I say.

I can't believe that Mackenzie doesn't want to be my partner, and what does she mean about sugar? This conversation is not going the way I planned.

The warning bell rings to let us know we have five minutes to get to homeroom, and the once crowded hallway starts to empty.

I try to find a way to calm things down.

"I'm so sorry you've been sick, Mackenzie," I say. "I really hope you come back to tennis. I'd love to be your partner if you'll play with me. Coach had me practicing with Lindsey while you were gone, and I did have fun, but I want to play with you too. I promise I won't say anything mean again or at least not on purpose. I feel really bad about how I acted."

Mackenzie looks like she's deciding whether to believe me or not. She grabs her math book and shuts her locker door, then turns back to face me.

"I'll be back to tennis practice today. When I passed out in the assembly, the school nurse snitched to my parents that I've been skipping tennis," she says. "My mom threatened to take away my phone and ear buds if I don't show up."

"Great! I'll see you at practice then," I say, glad that Mackenzie doesn't seem so angry. "We better get to class before the tardy bell rings. I swear I didn't mean what I said, and I promise I won't say anything mean about you again."

"Okay, I'll see you at practice," says Mackenzie. She picks up her book bag and starts heading in the opposite direction.

She didn't look like she totally believed me, but I feel relieved as I walk away from Mackenzie. I guess she was as upset about being my partner as I was about being hers. Maybe things will be better at our next practice.

Chapter 15

Dear Diary

More drama happened at tennis today, so I have a lot to write about in my diary this evening.

There's a rain storm outside, and the power is out, and we all go to bed early. I rummage around in my nightstand and pull out my portable reading light. Afterward, I roll down my bedspread and slide under the covers waiting for my parents to come in my room.

I would never tell my friends, but I still like my Mom and Dad to tuck me in, even though I'm in sixth grade.

"You sure you're not scared in here by yourself with the storm going on?" asks my mother. She's holding Dad's extra-bright flashlight and I cover my eyes so it doesn't blind me.

"Nah, I'm fine," I say. "I usually don't have my nightlight on so I'm used to it being dark."

"Okay, well you know we're just down the hall if you need us," says Dad, kissing me on the forehead.

"Mommy, Daddy, you coming?!!" Cole calls.

"Yes, your highness," says my mother with a laugh.

After my parents leave my room, I grab my journal from my nightstand, unlock it with the tiny attached key, and click on the portable light.

Dear Diary,

Mackenzie is back in tennis. She wouldn't tell Coach why she'd been absent for a week, and she didn't have a doctor's note, so he made the entire team run three extra laps as punishment for her skipping. Kennedy was especially mean to all the sixth graders afterward. I don't know how I thought I could be friends with her. Mackenzie didn't seem too mad at me during practice. She talked to me, and we had a good time playing together. I hope she doesn't get sick again.

Crack! Boom!!

A clap of thunder and a streak of lightning jolts me, and I drop my ink pen in my thick comforter.

"Where is that thing?" I search through the folds to find it.

I look up to see a huge shadow with a big square head looming on my wall.

"Cole, what are you doing in here?" I say to my little brother, who stands in the doorway in his pajamas.

"I can't sleep," he says.

"Why don't you get Mom and Dad?" I ask.

"They're not up, and Dad doesn't like me bringing Bertram in there."

Mmmm, Mmmm, Mmmm. Bertram pads in my room behind him, tilts his head, looks at me, and starts to whine.

"All right, come in, guys," I say.

The wind howls, and rain pounds down in sheets. I wonder if our backyard will flood. The last time it rained like this it looked like a swimming pool out there.

"Why are you doing homework this late?" Cole points at my journal.

"It's not homework. It's my diary, and it's my private business."

"Business? Are you making a lemonade stand or something?"

"No, silly, it's just my thoughts and feelings. Mom got it for me to write down things I do each day."

"Why do you want to write down your thoughts?" he says.

"When I feel bad or confused about something, writing it down helps me figure things out."

"Well, it sounds like homework to me," says Cole. "I hope Mom doesn't buy me a journal."

He plops down on my bed and sits beside me as we listen to the rain whoosh and splatter outside. I set my journal down. It's kind of nice having my little brother and Bertram here with me.

I sit on the edge of the bed and rub Bertram's fur while Cole curls up beside me, and think about today's tennis practice. Mackenzie showed up and we had a good time playing against Chloe and Mariama, even though we didn't win. The other girls were kind of irritated with her because we had to run laps as punishment for her skipping practice, and the coach showed no mercy.

"The nurse told me you fainted in assembly because you skipped breakfast," he said to Mackenzie in front of the team. "As an athlete you need to make sure you are eating properly and keeping in shape by attending regular practices. You missed five days of tennis practice last week with no approved excuse, so you're lucky I'm still letting you stay on the team."

"Look at her, acting like it's not her fault we have to run," grumbled Kennedy as the entire team had to do extra laps.

Mackenzie nervously twisted her bracelet around her arm and didn't say anything.

I turned to Kennedy. "Leave my partner alone," I said. "If you hadn't been so mean to everybody, maybe she wouldn't have ditched practice."

"Like you were any nicer to her," said Kennedy, putting her hands on her hips.

"You're right, I was just as bad as you are," I said. "But at least I learned my lesson and am not still being a jerk."

"Watch it, sixth grader," said Kennedy. "Don't forget that I'm team captain."

"Some captain," said Chloe. "We only have seven people on the team. There's not even anything for you to do."

"I'm not wasting any more time with you babies," said Kennedy. "This is a warning, Washington, watch your mouth." Kennedy picked up her duffle bag and stomped away.

"Don't worry about her, Sophie," said Chloe. "She's just running her mouth."

Mackenzie still didn't talk much to me, but she smiled as we all walked off the court. Maybe we can be the tennis partners I hoped we'd be.

Chapter 16

Match Day

It's our Match Day against St. Regis, and I'm queasy. This is my first time playing in a real sports game, and since she's missed so much practice, I'm not sure if Mackenzie and I are ready.

"You're going to do great, ladies!" Valentina cheers us on from the stands. Toby and Nathan sit beside her. If Coach hadn't told her fans should not be noisy during tennis matches, I wouldn't put it past Valentina to bring her cheerleading pom poms and megaphone out here. She still has a medical boot on her injured foot, so she can't get up and do any jumps or flips, thank goodness.

My Dad has to work late at his dentist office and can't make the game, but Mom and Cole are coming after they return from his class field trip to the zoo.

"MVP! MVP!" Toby and Nathan laugh. Those two have teased me since a ball bounced off my head at our first practice. They must not have gotten the memo from my coach about fans being quiet because they are not keeping the volume down.

"We've got your MVP," says Mackenzie to my surprise. "Come on, partner."

She puts her arms around my shoulder and leads me onto the court. We've had just two practices since she came back, but I can tell she's more into tennis. Instead of daydreaming when Coach Quakenbush gives instructions like she used to, she's been paying attention. Coach taught us how to give hand signals behind our backs when one person is standing at the net and the other is serving so we can secretly tell each other to switch sides of the court. Yesterday, we used the play to fake out Chloe and Mariama and actually beat them.

"Thanks for taking up for me back there with Nathan and Toby," I say. "I'm so happy you're feeling better and we're going to play our first real tennis match. I can't believe I'm this excited about being on a team. Are your parents coming to our game, Mackenzie?"

"Nah, they are both out of town so I'm staying with my nanny this week," she answers. "They made me be on the team because my doctor says I need to get exercise, but they probably will never see me play."

"What are their jobs?" I ask.

"My mom is an interior decorator and she decorates homes for people all over the country, and my father owns a fast food restaurant, so he's there working all the time," she answers.

"Wow, that sounds exciting," I say. "You probably get lots of goodies."

"Trust me, it seems more glamorous than it is," Mackenzie says. She wipes sweat off her forehead with her hand. "My mom and dad are hardly ever around, and I don't care if I never eat another French fry again."

We set our water bottles on the bench at the side of the court and prepare to warm up before the St. Regis team gets here.

"Let's practice our serves," I call to Mackenzie as she walks to the other side of the court.

"Okay, let me check something in my bag for a sec," she says. While she skips over to the benches by the chain-link fence, I practice popping a tennis ball in the air using alternate sides of my racket. Kennedy and Jacqueline walk up.

"Good luck, kiddies," says Kennedy with a flip of her braids. She and Jacqueline are on their way to warm up in the court beside us. I'm surprised she's still speaking to me after what happened the other day.

I wonder what is taking Mackenzie so long? I set down my tennis ball and glance over to the benches. She's sitting down, and her face even looks even paler than usual. I run over to her.

"What's wrong?" I ask.

"I dunno. I just feel funny all of a sudden," she says. "Like I'm gonna throw up." She bends over and holds her head in her hands. "I see dark spots!"

"Do you need some water?" I say in a panic.

What should I do?!! Is she going to pass out like she did in the assembly?

"Where's Coach?" I call over to Kennedy and Jacqueline.

"He went to get our water cooler." Kennedy catches the ball in her hand and glances over at our court. "Since I'm team captain, I'm in charge of warmups. What's up with Big Mac?"

"Her name is Mackenzie," I say.

"Well, her name is going to be lap runner if she doesn't get off that bench and start stretching for our match," says Kennedy.

"Can't you see she doesn't feel well?" I say.

"I'm all right," Mackenzie says weakly. "You don't have to call the coach." She leans back on the bench.

Not sure how to help, I fan her with my tennis racket.

"Are you trying to cool her off, Sophie?" calls Nathan from the bleachers behind the fence. "I don't think she'll get much air through all the holes in your tennis racket."

"Hey, MVP. I don't play tennis, but I think you might need to start warming up before the other team gets here," says Toby, trying to be

funny. "From what I saw last time we were out here you need plenty of practice."

"I guess you're right," I say with a fake smile and a nervous glance at Mackenzie. The boys are far enough away that they can't tell that anything is wrong.

"Are you getting sick?" I whisper to Mackenzie. "Are you going to faint again?"

"I'll be fine," she says. "I just need to sit here for a minute."

"You don't look so good," I say. "How are you going to play in our match? Maybe we should have the nurse come out."

"No!" says Mackenzie firmly.

I can tell she doesn't want anyone to notice she's not feeling well, but what if this is serious?

"Kennedy, we need help," I say.

"Okay," Kennedy says after walking over to our court and taking a closer look at Mackenzie. "You're right, Sophie, she does look funny. You're not going to pass out again, are you?"

"Can somebody *please* get the coach?" I say with a rise in my voice.

"Is everything okay out there?" My mother and Cole arrive at the bleachers, and she sets down a duffle bag.

"I'm not sure, Mom," I say.

She hurries out to the tennis courts and puts her hand on Mackenzie's forehead.

"This child looks terrible! Nathan and Toby,

run and get the school nurse. Do you have any kind of health problem that you know of, sweetie?" she asks Mackenzie.

Mackenzie doesn't answer. Her eyes are open, but it doesn't look like she knows what is going on.

"Thanks goodness, she has on a medical brace-let!" says my mother looking at her arm. She twists the bracelet around on Mackenzie's wrist and points out a design that looks like an x with a line through it and a snake wrapped around the line.

"This is the symbol for medical emergencies."

"So that's why she wears that bracelet all the time!" says Chloe. She, Mariama, Valentina, and the other girls on the team have made it over to our court as well.

"Go get a juice box from my bag, Sophie," says Mom. "I think your friend has diabetes."

Chapter 17

Forfeit

Mackenzie slurps down Cole's juice box and after a few minutes starts crying.

"It's all right, dear," says my mother. "There's no need to be upset. The color is back in your face, and you look much better. How do you feel?"

"A little bit better," says Mackenzie weakly. She leans with her head covered more out of embarrassment than being sick. Mom gestures for all of us to move a few feet away from the bench.

"How did Mackenzie get di-beeties, Mom?" Cole whispers, eyes big. "What does it mean?"

"After you eat, your body turns food into sugars, or glucose," Mom says. "The glucose is moved throughout your body by a hormone called insulin, and that gives you energy. When a person has diabetes, the insulin doesn't work as it should and the sugars stay and build up in their blood, which makes them sick. They have to take special medicine through pills or shots to give them the insulin they need to stay healthy."

"Is there a way to tell if a person has diabetes, Mom?" I ask.

"Is it contagious?" says Cole.

"Well, they might be thirsty a lot or have to rush to the restroom," she says. "Diabetes is not contagious, but it can run in families. People develop some forms of the disease from being overweight or eating certain foods. Sometimes diabetes can be managed through diet and exercise."

"Wow! You know as much as a doctor, Mrs. Washington!" says Chloe.

"My father had diabetes, and he sometimes would get sick if his body had a bad reaction to his medication or he didn't eat well," she says. "His blood sugar levels would shoot too high or too low and he would become weak and disoriented. Sadly, he never could follow the doctor's orders with his eating and exercise and got worse over time."

She goes back to the bench. "Can you walk now, Mackenzie? Let's get you to the school nurse."

"What's going on here?" Coach Quackenbush scurries quickly onto the court.

"Mackenzie just had a diabetes episode, and we gave her some juice," says Mom. "I'm taking her to the nurse's office so she can lie down until her parents come get her."

"Diabetes?! I wasn't aware of that," says Coach. "They do a terrible job of keeping medical records around here. All right. I'll take Mackenzie. It's safe for her to walk, right?"

"She should be okay now to get to the nurse's office," says Mom.

Mackenzie stands.

The coach turns to the tennis team members. "Singles players and number one doubles team, keep warming up. St. Regis will be here in about ten minutes. Unfortunately, we'll have to have you sit out this week, Sophie, and forfeit you and Mackenzie's game. Lindsey has been preparing to play singles all week, so I'm going to leave her in that spot."

Mackenzie wipes her eyes, and my mother gives her another hug.

"Man, this is awful!" says Jacqueline.

"Sorry I gave you such a hard time, Big...I mean Mackenzie," says Kennedy. "I hope you feel better soon."

Nurse Bloomberg, Toby, and Nathan arrive.

"I'll take over from here, Coach Quackenbush," says the nurse. "I have some insulin for Mackenzie in my office in case she needs it."

"I'm sorry I got sick, Sophie," says Mackenzie. "I know how excited you were about our first match."

"No worries," I say. "You can't help it if you don't feel well."

My chest feels tight as Mackenzie mopes off the tennis court behind Nurse Bloomberg. Diabetes is terrible. I didn't know my grandfather well since he died when I was just five years old. I remember crying every time he tried to hug me after he stayed in the hospital because afterward, one of his legs was missing. Seeing a stump where his long leg used to be scared me more than going to sleep without my nightlight.

My grandmother and other family members kept whispering about Paw Paw's "sugar," so I suppose diabetes had something to do with it. I hope that nothing bad like that happens to Mackenzie.

"Will Mackenzie be able to play tennis again, Mom?" I ask. "Or will she keep getting sick?"

"Nurse Bloomberg said she is getting used to taking her diabetes medicine on her own," says my mother. "When I gave her juice, Mackenzie told me she took an extra pill at lunchtime so that might have made her blood sugar too low. Once she is able to handle things properly, I'm sure she'll be able to come back to the team. Exercise is one of the best ways for her to stay healthy and manage her condition. I'm sorry you won't be playing today, Sophie. I was looking forward to seeing you in action."

"Yeah, I'm getting much better," I say. "Dad taught me some trick shots."

"I bet I can still beat you," says Cole.

"Yeah, right, Cole," I say. "You haven't beat me the first time."

"Let's go back to the benches; I'm tired of standing," says Cole. He looks over to the bleachers where the parents of our teammates are sitting. "Can we at least watch Chloe and Mariama's game?"

"That's a great idea," says Mom. "Come on kids."

Chapter 18

St. Regis

"Let the games begin," says my mother, plopping down in the bleachers. "Thanks for your help with getting the nurse, guys." She turns to Nathan and Toby. "I was expecting most of the excitement to happen during the tennis match, not beforehand."

"I'm so glad you got here when you did, Mom," I say. "Coach is always running around getting water or looking for his clipboards. I didn't know how to help Mackenzie."

"I'm sure that was scary, sweetie," says Mom. "I'm happy we could help her before she went into shock."

"I'm sorry about what happened to your partner, Sophie," says Nathan.

"Yeah, that's messed up," says Toby. "I feel bad about teasing you guys. I wonder why Mac never told anybody she was sick."

"She thought people would make fun of her about it," I say.

"The kids around here are kinda loco, but I doubt that would happen," says Valentina. She sits with her injured foot propped on the bleachers in front of us.

"Well, some of us have been mean to her so she probably didn't know," I say.

"The other team is coming to the gate!" says Cole. "Finally, we get to see some tennis."

The St. Regis girls look like they are heading to the U.S. Open. They all wear coordinated green and white uniforms and the same white, Nike brand tennis shoes.

Chloe and Mariama seem nervous as they meet the girls they are playing and move to their court to let them warm up. I've never seen Mariama jump around like that. Both the St. Regis girls are Asian, and they carry identical, fancy-looking tennis rackets. Their names, Cindy and Eileen, are embroidered on their polo shirts. Our team uniforms still haven't come in yet, but Chloe and Mariama are sharp in the matching white tennis outfits they bought at the mall. After about ten minutes of warm up, Chloe flips the racket for the serve. The rackets lands on the side the St. Regis girls picked, so they take the new can of tennis balls to begin the game.

"I've got another joke for you, Sophie," says Cole as the girl named Cindy tosses up the ball to serve it.

"What did one tennis ball say to the other tennis ball…see you round. Get it, tennis ball and round?" he says with a laugh.

Nathan and Toby join him in chuckling at the silly joke.

"Zip your lips!" I say. "I'm trying to watch the game."

'We're not in the library. We don't have to be quiet out here," says Cole.

"Yeah, Sophie. Who made you the noise police?" says Nathan.

"In tennis, it's good manners to be quiet when players are hitting the ball," says Mom. "It's fine to cheer a bit or move around in between points, but making a lot of noise during a match can make it hard for the players to do their best."

"Yeah, I've missed the last two points while your mouth was moving, Cole," I say.

"Cut it, Sophie," he answers.

While we are arguing, Chloe and Mariama rush to the net at the same time to hit a short ball that zooms toward the center line.

"Get it, guys!" I forget what I just told Cole about being quiet and shout out.

Mariama looks my way for a split second before she swings and misses the ball.

I clasp my hands over my mouth. "Oh no!"

Thankfully, Chloe swerves behind Mariama and scoops up the shot that her partner missed. The ball lobs high in the area over Cindy's head and bounces right on the line, winning Chloe and Mariama the point.

"That's my baby!" Chloe's mother, Mrs. Thompson, applauds.

"Way to go Xavier!" yells Valentina.

"She still thinks she's a cheerleader, even though she can't do a cartwheel with that broken foot," says Toby with a chuckle.

"I *know* I'm a cheerleader," says Valentina. "I have school spirit no matter what."

"I'm hungry. Can I get some popcorn at the concession stand?" asks Cole.

"Sure, son, and bring back some slushes too," says Mom, handing him a ten dollar bill.

"Make that two popcorns," I tell my brother.

"You look like Gru, but I'm not your minion," says Cole. "If you want popcorn, get it yourself."

"If I look like Gru, than you look like Yoda," I say, ready for battle.

"Oooo!" say Nathan and Toby, turning their heads back and forth between me and Cole like they are tracking a tennis ball.

"Cut it with the insults or neither of you is getting anything," says Mom.

"Yes, ma'am," Cole and I say at the same time. I can almost taste those salty, buttery, popcorn kernels and I don't want to miss out. When my mother tells us to stop arguing, she means business.

"Come on, Cole, let's hurry up so we don't miss anything." I stand and zigzag my way through the crowd on the bleachers, and he follows. The line is humongous because Xavier is also having baseball and softball games today.

"Will you quit bumping into me?!!" I fuss at Cole as he fidgets in the winding concession stand line we stand in. My stomach growls from the mixed smells of popcorn, cotton candy, and hot dogs.

"I wish they'd hurry up," Cole complains.

"No kidding," I say.

By the time we get back with two boxes of popcorn and three raspberry slushes, the tennis match is half over.

"That other team is cheating," says Valentina with a frown.

"Should we call the coach?" says Cole.

"What do you mean the ball is out?!" Chloe calls to the girls from the other team. "I saw it hit the line."

"It was just past the line," says Cindy, pointing her racket head beyond the baseline of the court.

"You need glasses," says Mariama. "That ball was in."

"I'm standing by the line and it was out." Cindy stands firm.

"I saw the ball hit the line too," Nathan says to my mother. "Is there anything we can do?"

"It's the other team's call in middle school tennis," says Mom with a shake of her head. "They

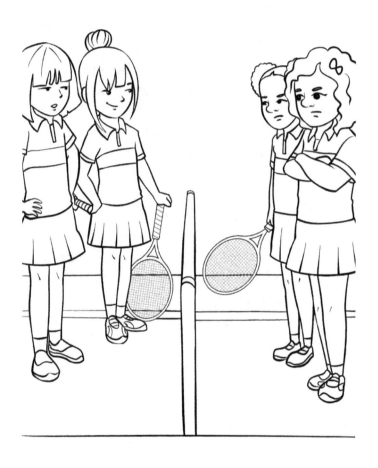

play on an honor system, so both teams need to be honest."

"That is so not fair," I say as the game continues.

"It's okay, Chloe's doing awesome," says Valentina as our friend springs through the air like a cobra and slams the ball at Eileen's feet.

"Wow! She's nearly as good at tennis as you are at basketball, Toby," says Nathan.

"Yeah, she is pretty good," Toby agrees.

"Is Chloe your girlfriend?" asks Cole, and Toby blushes.

"All right now, Mariama!" cheers Valentina when Mariama hits an "ace" serve that Cindy completely misses.

"I see you MVP!" yells Nathan.

We have so much fun laughing and cheering on our friends that I forget how disappointed I was at not being able to play. Despite St. Regis' early cheating, Chloe and Mariama win their match 6-3; 6-2, and the three singles teams win their games too.

"All right, great job, girls!" The coach calls us over for a brief team meeting once everything is over. "I know you complain about all the running and drills we do in practice, but now you see that they have a purpose. You were all winners today, and I couldn't be prouder. We'll take a break from practice tomorrow to rest up, but I'll see you all back on Monday after school, ready to work. All right, have a great weekend!"

"All right!" we answer back.

Coach doesn't say anything about Mackenzie. I wonder if he got an update from the nurse while the tennis match was going on. I remember Mom saying she should be fine by tomorrow. I'll call her in the morning to see how she's doing.

Chapter 19

Mac is Back

Dear Diary,

We had so much fun this weekend! Cole and Dad played basketball at the Rec Center on Saturday, and Mom took me to a Mother-Daughter tea at our church. We wore ruffled dresses, and Mom put on a floppy straw hat with a red flower on it. She styled my hair with a headband thingy called a fascinator that she says all the famous people wore to the Royal Wedding in England. The tea party was great! We ate little sandwiches with cream cheese and cucumbers in them and all kinds of fancy desserts. My favorites were the chocolate mousse cups with whipped cream on top. The mini strawberry cupcakes were good too. Chloe's family also goes to our church, and she and her mom were at our table. You should have seen the lacey yellow and green dress she had on! On Sunday, Mom cooked a big dinner after church with baked chicken and mashed potatoes.

Yum! Next, all four of us went on a bike ride in our neighborhood. Sometimes we see wild animals like alligators and ducks, but this time, none were around. So much was going on that I nearly forgot to call Mackenzie, but before bedtime, Mom got her home phone number from the Xavier Academy directory for me. Nobody answered when we called. I hope she's well now. I guess I'll find out at school today.

Come on, Sophie, we're going to be late!" Mom calls up to me from downstairs.

"On my way!" I yell from my room. I use my little key to lock up my diary and then bound down the stairs.

"Owww! That hurts!" Cole leans to the side in pain as Mom combs through his matted hair. "I can do it myself."

"If you'd do a better job of picking out your hair, I wouldn't have to bother with this," she says and shakes her head as Cole continues to squirm. "Keep this up, and I'm having your dad tell the barber to shave all this off at your next appointment."

"Noooo, I want to let my hair grow out!" says Cole.

Mom squirts some leave in conditioner on his hair to soften it. "This makes no sense. Don't you have a special program going on today? You need to look nice."

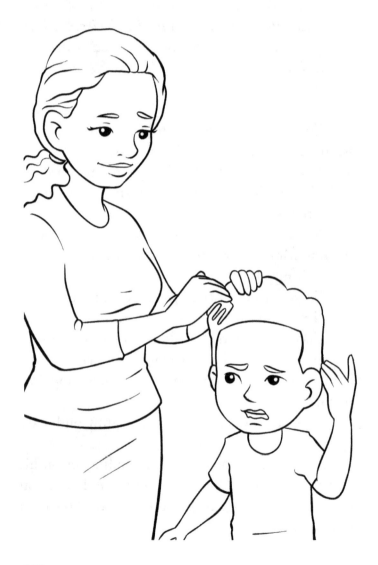

"We're having our art show," says Cole. He shrugs his shoulders in relief as Mom finishes up with his beauty treatment. "My teacher is hanging up our pictures this morning and I want to give her some extras I did at home." He points to his art portfolio case that holds his drawings that is sitting on the floor near his book bag.

"All right, Picasso, let's get going," I say as I pick up my backpack and tennis racket.

"I can't wait to see all the beautiful art you kids have created," says Mom. "I know how much work you put into everything, Cole."

"I'll be sure to stop by after work to see your painting on the wall, son," says my father, patting my brother's back on his way to the garage. "I've been telling everybody at my office about my young artist."

Cole beams.

"I'm proud of you, little bro," I add to the love fest.

"Okay, let's load up the car and get to it," says Mom. Dad pecks her on the cheek and pulls me and Cole in for a group bear hug. Bertram stands in the corner looking left out, so I slip him a dog biscuit before I follow my brother into the garage.

I'm in such a good mood from the weekend that I don't mind when Cole starts in with his usual chatter.

"I wonder why the sky is blue and not green like the grass?"

"That's a good question," I say, rather than telling him to Google the answer as I normally would. "I might ask my science teacher about it in class today."

"Wanna hear another tennis joke?" Cole takes advantage of my unusual patience.

"Sure," I sigh. "Let's have it."

"What's the name of a girl who stands in the middle of a tennis court?"

"What?"

"Annette."

"That's a good one, Cole," says Mom with a chuckle.

"Yeah, that joke isn't too bad," I say.

Cole starts looking over his art book and I stare out the car window for the final ten minutes of our ride to Xavier. I hope I see Mackenzie today, but I'm not sure what to say to her. She was so embarrassed about people knowing about her diabetes that I don't want to make a big deal about it.

I must have called Mackenzie up with my thoughts because as soon as we pull up to the school, I see her nanny's gray mini-van drive up behind us.

"Mackenzie is here!" I say with excitement to my mother. "She must be well now."

"What happened on Friday was probably a case of her taking too much of her diabetes medicine," says Mom. "I'm sure she should be fine. See you later, sweetie." She blows me a kiss.

Mom drops me off at the school entrance and then parks her car in the visitor's lot. The art show is going on all day today, and Mom's walking into the school with Cole this morning to see his painting. I may go over there after school if I have time before tennis practice, otherwise I can see it when he brings it home. The middle schoolers are kept separate from the lower grades, so my friends and I aren't allowed to go to their area without a teacher or parent.

"Hey, Mackenzie, wait up!" I call to my tennis partner as she walks toward the front door.

"Hi, Sophie," she answers. Her face is its usual chalky white color and not almost blue like it was on Friday, so I figure she's better.

"I was so worried about you, and I didn't have your number to call to see how you were doing," I say. "Is everything okay?"

"Yeah, the nurse said I took too much of my medicine," says Mackenzie. "I only need one pill for my insulin, but I took two because I sneaked and ate some cookies at lunch. I thought that the extra medicine would keep my blood sugar from going back up, but it didn't. I felt terrible. I won't do that again. My mom and dad were mad at me because the nurse had to call them away from their jobs."

"Everybody will be psyched to see you at practice today," I say. "We won the match against St. Regis, so Coach was happy."

"I'm sorry that my dumb mistake kept you from playing, Sophie," says Mackenzie. "I'll make it up to you at our next game."

"Mistakes aren't dumb as long as you learn from them," I say, repeating something my Granny Washington tells me.

"Hey, Sophie and Mac! Sup?!!" Toby greets us as we move down the hallway.

"Hola, Mackenzie. Good to see you back!" Valentina walks over carefully to keep her crutches from sliding on the floor. I'm sure she'll be glad to get that boot off her foot in three weeks.

"Thank you," Mackenzie says with a blush. "I'm not really happy to be in school, but I'm glad I'm not sick anymore. I appreciate you all thinking about me." She stops at the intersection of the entryway and the hallway where her locker is located. "I guess I'll see you at practice, Sophie. I need to get my books for first period."

"Okay, see you," I say.

My feelings toward my tennis partner have flipped 180 degrees. Before, I dreaded playing with her, now I can't wait. Mom says exercise helps people with diabetes do better, so if Mackenzie feels like she has friends on the tennis team she'll want to keep playing and that could help her become healthier. I don't want her to lose her legs when she gets older, like my granddad did. Win or lose, I decide she's the perfect match for me.

Chapter 20

Surprise

"I have a great idea to welcome Mackenzie back to the tennis team," I say to Chloe and Mariama. "A surprise party!"

We talk over the clang of metal in the sports locker room after school, changing into our practice uniforms and sneakers for tennis.

"Sounds good to me!" says Chloe. "I'm always up for a celebration."

"Would she like that?" says Mariama. "It doesn't seem like she wants a lot of attention."

"It would make her feel special," I say as I clip on my tennis visor. "Like everyone wants her on the team."

"Where would we have the party?" asks Mariama. "And what food would we eat? With her diabetes Mackenzie can't have anything sweet, can she? That means no cake or cookies."

"You're right, we shouldn't serve things with lots of sugar…" I stop to think.

"I know!" says Chloe. "We could use the recipes Dr. Wright gave us in assembly last week." She pulls the rumpled flyer out of her backpack. "I have a copy right here. I made the Banana Dog Bites after school one day, and they were really good. We can set out everything to eat on the bleachers.

"Awesome!" I say. "Do you have the recipes for the other foods they had at the assembly? We can make them too. I'll ask my mom if she can bring the snacks over after school so we don't have to store them here all day."

"We have some balloons and streamers at home," says Mariama. "I'll bring those for our decorations."

"This is gonna be great!" I pump my fist in the air.

"What are you little sixth graders so excited about?" Kennedy slides up behind us to get to her gym locker.

"We're planning a party for Mackenzie," I say.

"For what?" asks Kennedy. She pulls back her braids in a ponytail holder. "Not passing out? What's so wonderful about that?"

"We want her to feel welcome on the team," says Chloe. "Something you should be doing since you're the captain."

"As often as she misses practice, she's lucky she's still on the team," says Kennedy. "If you want to have a party, go ahead, but I'm not doing any planning."

She struts off to change into her shorts and t-shirt.

"Wow. I thought she was becoming nicer, but I guess not," I say.

"Never mind Kennedy, having a party is a great idea," says Chloe. "We'll ask Coach about it later."

During tennis practice, Mackenzie is full of energy. You'd never know that she had ever been sick.

"Take that!" she says, hitting the ball over Chloe and Mariama's heads.

"Out!" Makenzie holds her finger in the air to signal that the ball bounced past the line.

"Aww, man!" says Mackenzie with a laugh.

"Good try, partner." I pat her back.

"All right, ladies. Let's pick up tennis balls." We stop for a quick water break and then start scooping up wayward tennis balls with our rackets after Coach Quackenbush signals the end of practice. The entire team runs two laps around the courts and then we gather together near the gate.

"I was worried about you on Friday, Mackenzie," says the Coach. "But you did a great job today. You shouldn't have hidden the fact that you have diabetes. In the future, I'll make sure everyone's medical files are updated. Thank goodness Mrs. Washington was here on Friday and was able to help. We didn't know what was going on with you, and things could have been more serious."

"Yes, sir," says Mackenzie with her head down. She twirls her medical bracelet around her wrist.

"Coming, Sophie?" Mackenzie waits for me as I gather my backpack and tennis gear.

"Nah, I need to talk to Coach," I say.

She looks sad when I don't walk with her to the carpool area at the end of practice, but I want to ask Coach Quackenbush about the surprise party.

"All right, we can do it on Wednesday if you girls bring the food," he says after hearing my proposal. "But no eating until after practice. We're going to be doing lots of running to get ready for our next match."

"Thanks, Coach!" I say and then rush off to the parking area to find my mom.

"Where were you, Sophie?" asks Cole. "It's hot out here in the car. All your friends came out a long time ago."

"Sorry for making you wait," I say. "I was asking Coach Quackenbush if we can have a surprise party for Mackenzie to welcome her back on the team."

"That sounds like a sweet idea," Mom says. "When is this happening?"

"Wednesday after school, if it's all right with you," I say. "We want to make healthy snacks and bring them out after practice. I'd need you to help me get the cooler to school that morning, and Mariama says she might have some balloons we can use to decorate."

"You girls have really thought this out," says Mom. "I'm impressed."

"What about music?" says Cole. "I can make a Playlist on my iPad for you to use."

"Not just Radio Disney music," I say. "We like songs from the regular radio, too."

"I'll need to verify what's on the Playlist first to make sure it's acceptable," says Mom. "Thank you, Cole, for offering to help your sister."

"I thought the eighth graders would want to help us with planning, but Kennedy was being really mean about us having a party," I say.

"Even though she's older than you, she probably still has her own growing up to do," says Mom.

"Want to know how my art show went?" asks Cole, looking up from his video game handbook.

"Oh, yeah, I forgot about that," I say.

"It was super-duper, awesome!" says Cole. "Everybody loved my painting. It's a copy of *The Starry Night* by Vincent Van Gogh."

"That sounds cool, Cole. I can't wait to see it," I say.

"It's beautiful," says Mom. "I'm putting it on the wall in the dining room when you bring it home."

Another great ending to another great day, I think as we pull into the driveway at home. Wednesday can't come fast enough.

Chapter 21

Par-Tay

Dad would call our surprise tennis party for Mackenzie "awesome sauce." Chloe and Mariama came to my house after school on Tuesday and helped me get things prepped for the Banana Dog Bites, Guacamole and chips, and Apple Cinnamon Smoothies.

"This is going to be so fun!" said Chloe after scooping up a bite of guacamole on a chip.

"I didn't think I'd like this healthy stuff, but the food is pretty good," I say, helping myself to another sample.

"Let's put everything in the fridge so it'll be fresh for tomorrow," says Mom. "I'll bring all the snacks over right after school and Cole can help me set up while you girls get dressed for tennis."

"Thanks, Mom! You're the best." I smile and give her a hug.

"Well, I think it's very sweet of you girls to try to make Mackenzie feel more included on the team," says Mom.

"How do you like my party music?" asks Cole. He turns up the volume on one of my favorite songs and starts bouncing side to side to imitate the latest dance craze.

"Everybody will love it!" I say, joining him.

"Yeah, this song is the jam," says Chloe, moving to the beat.

"I wish I could make it to the event," says my father laughing as he enters the kitchen. "This is going to be quite the par-tay."

"I'll record some of it so you can catch all of our moves," says Cole, gliding across the floor.

The food and decorations turn out perfectly on the day of the party. There are a few clouds in the sky, so it's not too hot and the sun feels like a warm hug on my skin. Mackenzie doesn't notice Mom and Cole over by the bleachers.

"Let's hit some before Coach comes out and has us run more laps," she says.

"Sure," I say and wave at my mother when Mackenzie grabs two neon-yellow tennis balls from a bucket.

It's all I can do to keep from spilling the beans about the party. I'm so excited you'd think the surprise was for me.

Mariama and Chloe got Valentina, Nathan, and Toby to help fill up the balloons with a portable helium pump during their free period. They're bringing them out near the end of practice.

The eighth graders almost spoil my good mood.

"Hey, Sophie, I see your mommy came out to see her little baby again," says Kennedy, pointing toward the bleachers during our warmup. "Look, she's even putting plates out for your afterschool snack! What's that green stuff? Gerber baby food?"

"Leave Sophie alone, Kennedy," says Mackenzie.

"And what are you going to do to stop me, Big Mac?" Kennedy puts her hands on her hips. "Better save your breath before you pass out again."

I turn to face her.

"Leave my partner alone, you bully, or I'm telling the coach. You're the team captain, and you're supposed to be helping us get along, but all you've done since we joined the team is be mean to people."

"Whatever, sixth grader," Kennedy says with a smirk. "Come on, Jacqueline, let's go to the other court. We don't have time for baby talk."

"Oooo, you told her," says Mariama as Kennedy and Jacqueline move on.

"I don't see why Jacqueline and Lindsey hang out with her," says Chloe.

"I know," I say. "I'm glad she's going to high school next year and won't be back on the middle school tennis team."

"I agree, partner," says Mackenzie. She puts her hand out, and begins the motions of our special tennis hand shake and I follow along.

"You can do it!" I say, impressed.

"I've been practicing," Mackenzie says with a smile.

"Hey, Sophie, what *is* this green stuff?" Cole calls from the bleachers. He looks at the two pitchers of Apple Cinnamon Smoothie my mother set out and scrunches up his nose.

"A healthy and delicious drink," I say. "Want to try some?"

"Nah, I'll just have water;" he says.

"Your mom and brother have a huge picnic for you, Sophie," says Mackenzie. "Why so much food?"

"It's a treat for everyone on the team," I say.

"You're so lucky," says Mackenzie. "There's no way my mother would take off from her work to do something like that for me."

"Well, my mom is around more since she works with my Dad in his office," I say. "Your mother has to travel all around the country to do her decorating, doesn't she? I'm sure she'd rather be home more with you."

"I guess," says Mackenzie. "Sometimes it doesn't seem like it. Hey, look! There's Nathan and Toby coming with some balloons." She points to the path leading to the tennis court benches. "I wonder what's up with that?"

Toby and Nathan each carry a bunch of rainbow-colored helium balloons.

"Surprise!" shouts Valentina from the top of the bleachers. "The balloons are for you, Mackenzie!"

She looks confused.

Coach Quackenbush blows his whistle. "All right, practice is over ladies." He sets his clipboard on the bench near tennis court gates. "We're having a party to celebrate Mackenzie's good health and her return to the team."

"What! I can't believe this." Mackenzie face reddens, and she puts her hands over her mouth to hide her shy grin.

"I'm so happy to have you as my partner, Mackenzie," I say patting her on her back. "We're gonna have a great rest of the season!"

"I guess you little sixth graders are good for something," says Kennedy, grabbing one of the tortilla chips to munch. "This party is keeping us from running laps *and* getting us good food."

Cole turns on his music. "I don't know about you guys, but I'm ready to dance!" He moves his arms in a stiff robotic motion and then shimmies his legs. Toby and Nathan hop up to imitate him.

"Your little brother is a party animal, Sophie," says Chloe with a chuckle.

The eighth graders seem to like "baby" boys at least because they join in the dance party with Cole, Nathan, and Toby, and then Chloe and Mariama rush over to the group. Valentina claps her hands from the bleachers. If she didn't still have that boot on her leg, I'm sure she'd be right down here there with them.

Mom and Coach Quackenbush laugh at the scene.

"Come, on Mackenzie!" I grab her hand and pull her over to the rest of the kids.

"I really can't dance, but I'll give it a try," she says with a smile.

If anyone told me a few weeks ago that my tennis partner and I would be line dancing together I'd think they were crazy. Now, I wouldn't want to be on the team without Mackenzie. What started out as a mismatch, now feels like the perfect combination. A yellow and black butterfly flutters high in the trees as we move in time to the music, and my spirit feels just as free.

Dear Reader:

Thank you for reading *Sophie Washington: Mismatch.* I hope you liked it. If you enjoyed the book, I'd be grateful if you post a short review on Amazon. Your feedback really makes a difference and helps others learn about my books. I appreciate your support!

Tonya

P.S. Please visit my website at www.tonyaduncanellis.com to see videos about Sophie and learn about upcoming books (I sometimes give away freebies!). You can also join Sophie's club to get updates about my new book releases and get a **FREE** gift. Click here

Tennis Terms

Forehand - Hitting the ball by swinging the tennis racket palm-first.

Backhand - Hitting the ball with the back of the hand in front of the palm.

Lob - A ball that is hit high and deep into the opponent's court.

Volley - A ball that is hit in midair without bouncing on the ground.

Topspin - Hitting the ball so that it rotates forward as it's moving.

Serve - To hit the ball to begin play.

Baseline - The line marking each end of the court.

Forfeit - To surrender.

Love - A score of zero.

Dr. Wright's
Healthy Snacks

Want to try out some of the healthy snacks from Xavier Academy's Nutrition Assembly? Here are the recipes!

Green Apple Smoothie

Ingredients

> 1 cup (packed) baby spinach
> 3/4 almond milk or water
> 1/2 cup diced fresh Granny Smith apple
> 1 small frozen banana
> 1/2 cup frozen pineapple chunks
> 1 tablespoon lemon juice
> 1 tablespoon honey
> Handful of ice cubes

Directions

> Blend spinach, 1/2 cup almond milk or water in a blender until smooth. Add other ingredients and blend until smooth and creamy.

Enjoy!

Banana Dog Bites

Ingredients

2 peeled bananas
1/4 cup peanut or almond butter
2 tortillas

Directions

Spread peanut or almond butter on tortilla
Insert banana
Roll banana in tortilla and cut into bites

Enjoy!

Guacamole and Chips

Ingredients

3 ripe avocados
1/2 small onion, finely diced
2 Roma tomatoes, finely diced
3 tbsp fresh cilantro, diced
1 jalapeno pepper
2 garlic cloves
1/2 tbsp. salt
1 lime, juiced

Directions

Slice and peel the avocados and remove the pits.
Mash the avocado and mix in the other ingredients. Serve with unsalted tortilla chips.

Enjoy!

Books by
Tonya Duncan Ellis

Sophie Washington
Hurricane
By Tonya Duncan Ellis

Sophie Washington
Mission Costa Rica
By Tonya Duncan Ellis

Sophie Washington
Secret Santa
By Tonya Duncan Ellis

Sophie Washington
Code One
By Tonya Duncan Ellis

For information on all Tonya Duncan Ellis books about Sophie and her friends

Check out the following pages!

You'll find:

- Blurbs about the other exciting books in the Sophie Washington series

- Information about Tonya Duncan Ellis

Sophie Washington: Queen of the Bee

Sign up for the spelling bee?

No way!

If there's one thing ten-year-old Texan Sophie Washington is good at, it's spelling. She's earned straight one-hundreds on all her spelling tests to prove it. Her parents want her to compete in the Xavier Academy spelling bee, but Sophie wishes they would buzz off.

Her life in the Houston suburbs is full of adventures, and she doesn't want to slow down the action. Where else can you chase wild hogs out of your yard, ride a bucking sheep or spy an eight-foot-long alligator during a bike ride through the neighborhood? Studying spelling words seems as fun as getting stung by a hornet, in comparison.

That's until her irritating classmate, Nathan Jones, challenges her. There's no way she can let Mr. Know-it-All win. Studying is hard when you have a pesky younger brother and a busy social calendar. Can Sophie ignore the distractions and become Queen of the Bee?

Sophie Washington: The Snitch

There's nothing worse than being a tattletale...

That's what ten-year-old Sophie Washington thinks until she runs into Lanie Mitchell, a new girl at school. Lanie pushes Sophie and her friends around at their lockers and even takes their lunch money.

If they tell, they are scared the other kids in their class will call them snitches and won't be their friends. And when you're in the fifth grade, nothing seems worse than that. Excitement at home keeps Sophie's mind off the trouble with Lanie.

She takes a fishing trip to the Gulf of Mexico with her parents and little brother, Cole, and discovers a mysterious creature in the attic above her room. For a while, Sophie is able to keep her parents from knowing what is going on at school. But Lanie's bullying goes too far, and a classmate gets seriously hurt. Sophie needs to make a decision. Should she stand up to the bully or become a snitch?

Sophie Washington: Things You Didn't Know About Sophie

Oh, the tangled web we weave...

Sixth grader Sophie Washington thought she had life figured out when she was younger, but this school year everything changed. She feels like an outsider because she's the only one in her class without a cell phone, and her crush, new kid Toby Johnson, has been calling her best friend Chloe. To fit in, Sophie changes who she is. Her plan to become popular works for a while, and she and Toby start to become friends.

Between the boy drama, Sophie takes a whirlwind class field trip to Austin, Texas, where she visits the state museum, eats Tex-Mex food, and has a wild ride on a kayak. Back at home, Sophie fights off buzzards from her family's roof, dissects frogs in science class, and has fun at her little brother Cole's basketball tournament.

Things get more complicated when Sophie "borrows" a cell phone and gets caught. If her parents make her tell the truth what will her friends think? Turns out Toby has also been hiding something, and Sophie discovers the best way to make true friends is to be yourself.

Sophie Washington: The Gamer

40 Days Without Video Games? Oh No!

Sixth-grader Sophie Washington and her friends are back with an interesting book about having fun with video games while keeping balance. It's almost Easter, and Sophie and her family get ready to start fasts for Lent with their church, where they give up doing something for forty days that may not be good for them. Her parents urge Sophie to stop tattling so much and encourage her second-grade brother, Cole, to give up something he loves most—playing video games. The kids agree to the challenge but how long can they keep it up? Soon after Lent begins, Cole starts sneaking to play his video games. Things start to get out of control when he loses a school electronic tablet he checked out without his parents' permission and comes to his sister for help. Should Sophie break her promise and tattle on him?

Sophie Washington: Hurricane

#Sophie Strong

A hurricane's coming, and eleven-year-old Sophie Washington's typical middle school life in the Houston, Texas suburbs is about to make a major change. One day she's teasing her little brother, Cole, dodging classmate Nathan Jones' wayward science lab frog and complaining about "braggamuffin" cheerleader Valentina Martinez, and the next, she and her family are fleeing for their lives to avoid dangerous flood waters. Finding a place to stay isn't easy during the disaster, and the Washington's get some surprise visitors when they finally do locate shelter. To add to the trouble, three members of the Washington family go missing during the storm, and new friends lose their home. In the middle of it all, Sophie learns to be grateful for what she has and that she is stronger than she ever imagined.

Sophie Washington: Mission: Costa Rica

Welcome to the Jungle

Sixth grader Sophie Washington, her good friends, Chloe and Valentina, and her parents and brother, Cole, are in for a week of adventure when her father signs them up for a spring break mission trip to Costa Rica. Sophie has dreams of lazing on the beach under palm trees, but these are squashed quicker than an underfoot banana once they arrive in the rainforest and are put to work, hauling buckets of water, painting, and cooking. Near the hut they sleep in, the girls fight off wayward iguanas and howler monkeys, and nightly visits from a surprise "guest" make it hard for them to get much rest after their work is done.

A wrong turn in the jungle midway through the week makes Sophie wish she could leave South America and join another classmate who is doing a spring break vacation in Disney World.

Between the daily chores the family has fun times zip lining through the rainforest and taking an exciting river cruise in crocodile-filled waters. Sophie meets new friends during the mission week who show her a different side of life, and by the end of the trip she starts to see Costa Rica as a home away from home.

Sophie Washington: Secret Santa

Santa Claus is Coming to Town

Christmas is three weeks away and a mysterious "Santa" has been mailing presents to sixth grader Sophie Washington. There is no secret Santa gift exchange going on at her school, so she can't imagine who it could be. Sophie's best friends, Chloe, Valentina, and Mariama guess the gift giver is either Nathan Jones or Toby Johnson, two boys in Sophie's class who have liked her in the past, but she's not so sure. While trying to uncover the mystery, Sophie gets into the holiday spirit, making gingerbread houses with her family, helping to decorate her house, and having a hilarious ice skating party with her friends. Snow comes to Houston for the first time in eight years, and the city feels even more like a winter wonderland. Between the fun, Sophie uncovers clues to find her secret Santa and the final reveal is bigger than any package she's opened on Christmas morning. It's a holiday surprise she'll never forget!

Sophie Washington
Code One

Anything Boys Can Do Girls Can Do Better!

Xavier Academy is having a computer coding competition with a huge cash prize! Sixth grader Sophie Washington and her friend Chloe can't wait to enter with their other classmates, Nathan and Toby. The only problem is that the boys don't think the girls are smart enough for their team and have already asked two other kids to work with them. Determined to beat the boys, Sophie and Chloe join forces with classmates Mariama, Valentina, and "brainiac," Rani Patel, to form their own all-girl team called "Code One." Computer coding isn't easy, and the young ladies get more than they bargain for when hilarious mishaps stand in their way. It's girls versus boys in the computer coding competition as Sophie and her friends work day and night to prove that anything boys can do girls can do better!

About the Author

Tonya Duncan Ellis was the most valuable player of her high school tennis team. She's author of the Sophie Washington book series which includes: *Queen of the Bee, The Snitch, Things You Didn't Know About Sophie, The Gamer, Hurricane, Mission: Costa Rica, Secret Santa, Code One,* and *Mismatch.* When she's not writing, she enjoys reading, swimming, biking and travel. Tonya lives in Houston, TX with her husband and three children.